HELLENIC STUDIES SERIES 98

BLEMISHED KINGS

T0311283

Recent Titles in the Hellenic Studies Series

Imagined Geographies in the Mediterranean, Middle East, and Beyond

A Monument More Lasting than Bronze
Classics in the University of Malawi, 1982-2019

Poetry and the Polis in Euripidean Tragedy

TA-U-RO-QO-RO
Studies in Mycenaean Texts, Language and Culture in Honor of
José Luis Melena Jiménez

Love in the Age of War
Soldiers in Menander

The Purpled World
Marketing Haute Couture in the Aegean Bronze Age

*Greek Media Discourse from Reconstitution of
Democracy to Memorandums of Understanding*
Transformations and Symbolisms

Euripides' Ino
Commentary, Reconstruction, Text and Translation

Greek Language, Italian Landscape
Griko and the Re-storying of a Linguistic Minority

Lovers of the Soul, Lovers of the Body

Audible Punctuation
Performative Pause in Homeric Prosody

Who Am I?
(Mis)Identity and the Polis in Oedipus Tyrannus

Demetrios of Scepsis and His Troikos Diakosmos
Ancient and Modern Readings of a Lost Contribution to Ancient Scholarship

Homer's Thebes
Epic Rivalries and the Appropriation of Mythical Pasts

The Cypria

Homeric Imagery and the Natural Environment

Achilles Unbound
Multiformity and Tradition in the Homeric Epics

http://chs.harvard.edu/chs/publications

BLEMISHED KINGS

SUITORS IN THE *ODYSSEY*, BLAME POETICS, AND IRISH SATIRE

Andrea Kouklanakis

Center for Hellenic Studies
Trustees for Harvard University
Washington, DC
Distributed by Harvard University Press
Cambridge, Massachusetts, and London, England
2023

Blemished Kings: Suitors in the Odyssey, Blame Poetics, and Irish Satire
By Andrea Kouklanakis
Copyright © 2023 Center for Hellenic Studies, Trustees for Harvard University
All Rights Reserved.
Published by Center for Hellenic Studies, Trustees for Harvard University,
    Washington, DC.
Distributed by Harvard University Press, Cambridge, Massachusetts and
    London, England
Printed by Gasch Printing, Odenton, MD
Cover Design: Joni Godlove
Production: Jen Jackowitz

ISBN: 978-0-674-27848-6
Library of Congress Control Number: 2023933712

Contents

Acknowledgments vii

Introduction 1

1. Greek and Irish Framework 7

1.1 The View from Irish Satire 7

1.2 Ancient Scholarship: Aristotle on Blame Poetry and the *Margites* 13

1.3 The View from Pindar: Reproachful Language 17

1.4 The View from Archilochus: Suitors, Iambic Poetry, and
Irish Satire 19

2. The Bold, the Satirist, the *Nēpios* 23

2.1 Thersites, Suitors, and the Language of Reproach 23

2.2 Suitors, Makers of Satire 30

2.3 Telemachus *Nēpios*, or "Sometimes I Feel like a Fatherless Child" 35

3. The Suit 41

3.1 Wooing and Contesting: The Institution of Courtship 41

3.2 Wrongful Wooing 52

4. Blame and Blemish 59

4.1 *Mōmon Anapsai*: Internal Evidence 59

4.2 *Mōmos* and *Mōlōps*: The Greek Evidence for Satirical Poets and
Blemished Kings 67

4.3 *Mōmos* and *Mōmeuō*: Begrudging and Gluttony 73

4.4 *Pharmakos*: Scapegoats and Sacrifice 76

4.5 *Mōmos* and *Aitia*: Origin of Trouble 80

4.6 *Mōmeuein* and *Nemesis*: The Talk of the People 81

4.7 *Polu Prōton*, *Polutropos*: Ruler in Contest and Speech 85

Contents

Conclusion 87

Bibliography 89

Index of Non-Engish Words 97

Subject Index.. 101

Acknowledgments

I wish to thank the people who have made this book project possible. I gratefully thank my dear mentor and friend, Francis Jones, Professor of Classical Greek Literature and Professor of Comparative Literature at Harvard University, and longtime director at Harvard's Center for Hellenic Studies in Washington DC, Gregory Nagy. Professor Nagy's colossal intellect and encouragement animated my studies, and I am in the company of the fortunate few who have worked with him and have watched themselves rise higher than they thought possible. Greg's guidance and words of praise are truly transformative. I thank the wonderful Emma Dench, Harvard's Dean of the College of Arts and Sciences and McLean Professor of Ancient and Modern History and of the Classics, for her piercing intelligence, mentorship, sense of humor, and continued words of support. I thank Harvard Eliot Professor of Greek Literature David Elmer for reading earlier versions of this work, and for offering critical feedback with finely pointed observations.

I thank supporters and friends of this work, especially Mary Ebbott, Professor of the Classics at the College of the Holy Cross in Massachusetts. Mary has been an unwavering long-time friend and has always cheered for the completion of this project with grace and sweetness. I am immensely grateful to the entire publications committee, editorial board, and productions managers at Harvard's Center for Hellenic Studies for including my book in this series. I would like to mention those with whom I had direct contact for their generosity, guidance, and help—Casey Dué for the prompt acceptance of this book, Mary Ebbott for opening paths, Professor Emeritus at Brandeis University, Leonard Muellner, for his kindness and communication over the years, Jill Curry Robbins, Production Manager for Print Publications, Charlotte Houghton, Publications Assistant, and Noel Spencer, Production Manager for Online Publications, for their welcoming words and work. I want to extend a hearty appreciation to Elizabeth Gibson, graduate student at Harvard University, for reading my work and offering her expertise on all the Irish side of my studies. I also thank Lahney Preston-Matto, Professor of English at Adelphi University and editor of *Eolas: The Journal of the American Society of Irish Medieval Studies*, for listening to an early presentation of this work and showing enthusiasm for the comparative approach. I thank the anonymous readers, and editors for their sharp eyes, and critical observations.

I wish to acknowledge Ronnie Ancona, mentor, friend and Professor Emerita of the Classics at Hunter College, at the Graduate Center at CUNY, and long term editor of *The Classical Outlook* journal. Professor Ancona has been instrumental for the development of my scholarly life and has shown continued friendship and support of this and other research endeavors. I offer a posthumous mention of gratitude to Dr. Orlando Marques de Paiva, Dean of the University of São Paulo in Brazil (1973-1977) in whose company I spent great part of my childhood. Dr. Orlando Paiva opened many avenues early on.

I thank my family—my daughters, Jolein and Laila, and my son, Leo. I give special thanks to my husband, Gregory Hoge, for always believing I could do this work, and for all his help in big and small ways even during a challenging medical residency training in the middle of the Covid-19 pandemic. Finally, I dedicated this book to my parents, Andreas Kouklanakis†, and to my mother, Maria Aparecida Vilela, who would have pursued their own intellectual curiosities if they had encountered the same opportunities I did. From them I inherited strength, perseverance, a love of knowing and living.

Introduction

The language of the suitors in the *Odyssey* reflects the power struggle for kingship in Ithaca; it is contentious, censorious, and abusive. Penelope's suitors, though kings (*basileis*) of their towns, are eager to become the king of Ithaca.[1] To that end, they not only need to marry Penelope, but also need to eliminate Telemachus, the rightful heir to the kingship (*Odyssey* 16.448). Their intent is to permanently blame and blemish the would-be king as unfit for kingship, and they hatch a plan to ambush and kill Odysseus' son. Although the suitors' blame speeches are articulated to cause injury, in the end (and in keeping with other reversals in the narrative), it is the suitors who will be fatally blemished, thus disqualified as candidates for the kingship of Ithaca.

I interpret this poetics of blame as Homeric expressions of reproach and critique against unsuitable kings. My aim is to identify, analyze, and contextualize these expressions of depreciation, most significantly, the phrase *mōmon anapsai*, traditionally translated as "to fasten blame" (*Odyssey* 2.86). This phrase is used by the most prominent suitor, Antinous, and is critical for my discussion. I further suggest that this poetics of blame depends upon an ideology whose premise rests on the notion that kings are either perfect (suitable), or imperfect (unsuitable). Such a premise highlights the suitors' intricate role as both

---

[1]   Some suitors are local to Ithaca (*Odyssey* 16.124). The designation of *basileis* for the suitors must be understood as a title of rank, such as "prince" or "chief." These men are referred to as the *herma poléos*, "mainstay of the city," and the *aristoi*, "the best" (*Odyssey* 23.121). For the purpose of my analysis, it is not critical to address the various distinctions associated with the term *basileus*, except to say that in the *Odyssey* we find the distinction between Greek kings and divinely ordained kings. Thus, Odysseus is righteous and fair in deed and word, "neither doing nor speaking beyond what is ordained among the people": οὔτε τινὰ ῥέξας ἐξαίσιον οὔτε τι εἰπὼν / ἐν δήμῳ (*Odyssey* 4.690), in contrast to "what is the custom among divine kings": ἥ τ' ἐστὶ δίκη θείων βασιλήων (*Odyssey* 4.691), a possible reference to kings in the East. Compare, for example, *basileus anēr* used of Odysseus as "royal-looking" and "strong and tall" (*Iliad* 3.166–170); *basileuteros*, of Agamemnon, "more royal," that is, higher in rank (*Iliad* 9.160, 392; *Odyssey* 15.533); *basileutatos*, of Agamemnon, "most kingly" (*Iliad* 9.69); *basileus*, of the sceptered king on the shield of Achilles (*Iliad* 18.556); *basilēes*, "prince," "chief" of the suitors (*Odyssey* 1.394; compare with 8.390). According to Aristotle kingship in heroic times was legal and hereditary, granted with the willing consent of the subjects in recognition of a first benefactor in the ancestral line (*Politics* 3.1285b5–9). This *basileus* had supreme command over matters of war, religious sacrifices, and lawsuits (*Politics* 3.1285b10–11).

imperfect kings and blame poets (satirists) of the rightful king; each of them desires to become the ruler of Ithaca.

As I examine the poetics of blame in the *Odyssey* in the context of royal appreciation and depreciation, that is, the relationship between praise, blame, and kingship, I have looked toward the regulatory role of Irish satire (*áer*) in early Irish law and myth as a fruitful comparandum. In an earlier comparative study of praise and blame in the Indo-European poetic tradition, *Servius et La Fortune*, Dumézil interprets the Indic and Roman poetic modes as royal appreciation (praise) on the one hand, and the Irish poetic mode as depreciation (blame, satire) on the other hand:

> L'Irlande, qui présente ainsi des traits archaïques dans le mode d'acquisition du pouvoir royal, n'aurait-elle pas gardé un mythe equivalent à ceux de Pṛthu et de Servius … ? Il nous semble que ce mythe existe en effet, mais dans une forme inattendue, en negative, "*l'appréciation qualifiante*" se realisant en *blâme* et *non en louange* et aboutissant non à un avènement mais à une deposition*, le poète appreciateur* fonctionnant comme *satiriste*, comme auteur de la première satire, et non comme panégyriste et inventeur de la louange, *la disette et l'avarice* avec leurs inconvénients se substituent comme *ressort de tout le drame aux beautés de l'abondance et de la générosité*—bref le mythe visant à établir sa leçon indirectement, par le spectacle des risques que comporte une transgression des règles, et non directement, par l'étalage des heureux résultats qu'entraîne le respect des règles.

> Ireland, which presents archaic traits in terms of acquisition of power, has it not preserved an equivalent myth to those in the Pṛthu and in Servius … It seems to us that this myth does in fact exist but in an unexpected form, as a negative, that is, the appreciation (appraisal) of qualification takes place in blame not in praise, and in leading not to the advent (coronation) of the king but to his deposing. The appraising poet functions as a satirist, as the author of the first [primal] satire, and not as a panegyrist and inventor of praise; shortage and avarice with their inconveniences are substituted in place of the beauty of abundance and generosity—in short, the myth aims at establishing its lesson indirectly by showing risks involved in the transgression of rules, and not directly, by the display of happy results that entail the respect for the rules.

> Dumézil *Servius et la Fortune* 230

One implication of Dumézil's observation is that the Irish poet's primary role was to compose satire (Irish: *áer*) rather than panegyric (Irish: *molad*), thereby to seek to depose a king who transgressed social contract rather than to praise one for upholding the good. Considerable scholarly work on the role of the poet (Irish: *fili*) in early and medieval Ireland has been added to the body of studies on praise, satire, law, regulation, and poetry since Dumézil's analysis.[2] Altogether, the evidence shows that the Irish poetic tradition encompassed the full spectrum between praise and blame, and that praise was in fact one of the primary functions of the poet.[3] Legitimate Irish satire was not only the negative side of praise, but also a form of poetic expression with crucial social function serving as a powerful incentive toward lawful behavior and as a deterrent against unlawful behavior in the early Irish system of justice.[4] Therefore, we should move away from Dumézil's evaluation of the makers of satire (and praise) as a "scourge" (Irish: *fléau*).[5]

Moreover, in Irish satire it mattered whether a person (a king, for example) deserved or did not deserve blame. This distinction is critical for assessing the legitimacy of the satire. In other words, poets should not use satire as a means of extortion, but rather as a system of justice functioning as a kind of checks and balances. If a satire was unjustly made, it should and could be remedied by praise (*molad do-nig áir*, "praise which washes away satire").[6] If justly made, it could be delivered as a cautionary warning: "A composition combining elements of praise and satire served a particular purpose—namely that of warning a person of an impending full satire [*sic*], was known as a *trefocal*, and formed an essential part of the process of lawful satirising ... The threefold division is reflected

---

2   See Kelly 1988; Breatnach 2006:63–84.

3   A critical issue concerning the composition of the praise poem in Irish writing is the relative scarcity of praise poems compared to satire in the pre-Norman period. This situation led scholars to associate the role of the poet in early modern Ireland primarily with the composition of satire. However, there is evidence that there was no fixed role for the *fili* as either satirist or a praise poet: "Not only is there a consistent connection made between praise and satire, but both are also associated with the *fili* as opposed to bard" (Breatnach 2006: 67). Breatnach points to the etymology of *fili* in Sanas Cormaic: **Fili** .i. fí anǽir & lí amolad in fili. Fili din .i. fialshúi. sái. fhéile, 'poet: "venom in the satire and splendour in praise of the poet" (67).

4   Kelly 1988:49–51; 137–139. Breatnach (2006:63–84) discusses the formulation of praise versus satire in the law tracts in *Bretha Nemed Dédenach*, where we find the question: *Cis lir a cenéla? .i. aí ⁊ anaí .i. áer ⁊ molad*, "How many are its varieties? i.e. poetry and un-poetry, i.e. satire and praise" (64). In addition, Breatnach highlights the fact that compositions in early texts themselves could present praise and satire in ambiguous terms, as the following assertion also in *Bretha Nemed Dédenach*: *Atá éolus ingnad lasna fileda .i. áer co ndath molta 7 mola co ndath aíre*, "The poets have remarkable expertise, i.e. satire with appearance of praise, and praise with appearance of satire" (66).

5   Dumézil 1943:236–237.

6   Breatnach 2006:65–66.

in the distinction made between the three colours of poetry."[7] This flexibility in the articulation of the binary praise-satire would allow the victim of satire to correct whatever behavior (typically a refusal) had incurred the satire in the first place.[8] Therein we see that there is a spectrum between the polarities of praise and blame, and not every satire was damaging or irreversible. These complications include the consequence that an unjust satire could not only incur an honor-price payment to the injured party, but it could also rebound on the poet delivering it.[9] To put it differently, if the satire is justified, then the bad ruler will be blemished; but if the satire is unjustified (i.e. poet-satirist is unfair and ruler does not deserve it), then the blemishes could be inflicted on the poet himself. Still, based on the power of the poets, all rulers (even good and generous ones) would have good reason to be afraid of poets and their satire.

I am interested in satire that poets make against those who fall short, rather than praise toward those who meet their obligation. Specifically, I am concerned with the consequences and effects of satire on its victim, that is, the blemishes (Irish: *boulgae*) that satire may cause on a person's face, notably rulers. In the *Odyssey* there is linguistic and semantic evidence pointing to blemishes as grounds for royal disqualification. Penelope's suitors are kings (*basileis*) seeking to disqualify Telemachus from obtaining kingship. The suitors make satire both against Telemachus and the hero-king himself, Odysseus, disguised as a beggar (the social reversal of a king). As such, they use epic language to mar his reputation, but in the end will become victims of their own satire.[10] In turn, various characters in the *Odyssey* continuously reproach the suitors, disqualifying any of them from becoming the king of Ithaca upon marrying Penelope.

I hope to show that the suitors offer the Greek illustration for what Dumézil calls *des traits archaïques dans le mode d'acquisition du pouvoir royal* ("archaic traits in the mode of acquisition of royal power") by comparing the social and political implication of their insults with Irish satire. Blame discourse in the *Odyssey* is informed by traits of struggle for royal power, fitting for a discussion centered

---

[7]   Breatnach 2006:66–67: "Those are the three colours of poetry, i.e. white, black, and speckled. White by which one praises, black by which one satirizes, speckled by which one give notice" The Irish concept of the three colors of poetry (*trefocal*) is analogous to the more inclusive meaning of the Greek *ainos* ("admonition") which I will discuss more at length below) to the Irish concept of three colors.

[8]   Breatnach 2004:25–36.

[9]   Néide was punished after making an unjust satire against Caier, king of Connacht (Stokes 1862: xxxvi–lx). See also the satire against King Bres in *Cath Maige Tuired* (Fraser 1916) and Dállan's satire against Áed in *Tromdámh Guaire* (Joynt 1941). For their unjust satires both Néide and Dállan meet their death.

[10]   King Conchobar mac Nessa destroys Athirne and his son ("the lustful poets") for desiring Luaine (Conchobar's wife to be), and for making a satire against her when she refused them (Stokes 1903: 270–285). Likewise does Odysseus destroy Penelope's lustful suitors.

on Penelope's suitors. I am looking at how Irish satire (*aér*), with its magical power to cause physical blemishes (*ainim*, *ferb*, *boulgae*) on the face of its victim, compares and applies to my observations about the suitors and phrase *mōmon anapsai* in its physical meaning as 'setting a brand'. As I have indicated above, in law tracts and in epic myth, "satire" (*áer*) can be made justly or unjustly. If the satire is just, that is, the ruler indeed falls short of his position), the cutting words carry the magical power not only to ruin that ruler by bringing failure to his affairs, but also by disfiguring his face with blemishes, a disqualifying mark:[11]

> L'éloge, *molad*, et la satire, *air* [=*áer*], ont sans doute l'un et l'autre un action magique, mais celle de la satire est de beaucoup la plus célèbre ... Depuis le satiriste, qui par un couplet (*glam dicend*) décoché, couvre de *pustule*[12] un royal visage (*fogeib teora boulga for a agaidh dosgene ind aor* ...) jusqu' à celui qui frappé de stérelité les champs et les arbres d'un royaume, cette engeance est un vrai fléau, plus dangereux, puisqu'elle dispose de forces magique, que le sycophante d'Athènes et ailleures, cette autre déformation pathologique du censeur.[13]

> Praise (*molad*) and satire (*áer*) both undoubtedly have magical effects, but the effect of satire is much more popular ... Whether it is from the satirist who by a magic spell covers with blemishes the royal face, or from the one who renders the field and the trees infertile, this brood [of satirists] is a scourge, even more dangerous than the sycophant of Athens and elsewhere, since it [the brood of satirists] has magical powers, which is another pathological deformity of the censor.

> Dumézil *Servius et la Fortune* 236–237

Thus, by looking at early and medieval Irish poetry I appropriate the term for satire—*áer*—and apply it to the Greek context, signaled by *mōmon anapsai* at *Odyssey* 2.86. And here I cite Marcel Detienne's *Masters of Truth*[14] where he

---

[11] I will discuss two notorious examples of satire followed by blemishes: the story of Caier and Néide (Stokes 1862: xxxvi-lx); and *The Wooing of Luaine* (Stokes 1903:270-285). Stokes (1903: 270) writes: "The tale [= *The Wooing of Luaine*] belongs to the Conchobar-cycle of romance, and turns on the Irish belief in the supernatural power of offended poets." It thus affords a parallel to the story of Néide and his uncle Caier [= Gaire] as told in Cormac's *Glossary*."

[12] Compare the entry for Irish *ferb* in Stokes (1862: xix, 19; with translation in Stokes 1868) which I discuss in more detail below.

[13] As I mentioned above, Dumézil's negative evaluation of Irish satirists as a "scourge" does not accurately describe the full role of the poet.

[14] Detienne 1973:18-27.

analyzes the inversely complementary nature of *epainos* (praise) and *mōmos* (blame). Detienne's study laid the foundation for the inclusion of the Greek poetic tradition within a paradigm of "Truth" as memory (*alētheia*), and "Falsehood" as forgetfulness (*lēthe*), that is, of understanding the absence of praise as "Blame" (*mōmos*). As I have mentioned above, satire can serve as socially constructive criticism and even restorative justice as it points out dangerous lapses and breaches of social contract.

1

Greek and Irish Framework

1.1 The View from Irish Satire

The suitors in the *Odyssey* speak in abusive and threatening language. They are presented as insulting, ungenerous, even wicked. They are arrogant, gluttonous, and their language is meant to undercut anyone who dares to criticize them, especially Telemachus. They transgress all norms of wooing and hospitality, and they threaten neither to leave the palace nor to stop consuming the livestock until Penelope chooses one of them. Their verbal threats are meant to disqualify Telemachus as the rightful king of Ithaca, and as I intend to show, the phrase *mōmon anapsai* encapsulates their threats. In addition, they are exceedingly numerous (an epic monstrosity in its own right), and Telemachus feels compelled to put up with them until Odysseus returns. Their behavior is in stark contrast to that of praiseworthy rulers. In book 19, Penelope questions Odysseus, who is still in disguise, and the hero compliments Penelope by comparing her fame to a "king free of blemish":[15]

> ὦ γύναι, οὐκ ἄν τίς σε βροτῶν ἐπ' ἀπείρονα γαῖαν
> νεικέοι· ἦ γάρ σευ κλέος οὐρανὸν εὐρὺν ἱκάνει,
> ὥς τέ τευ ἢ <u>βασιλῆος ἀμύμονος</u>, ὅς τε θεουδὴς
> ἀνδράσιν ἐν πολλοῖσι καὶ ἰφθίμοισιν ἀνάσσων
> εὐδικίας ἀνέχῃσι, φέρῃσι δὲ γαῖα μέλαινα
> πυροὺς καὶ κριθάς, βρίθῃσι δὲ δένδρεα καρπῷ,
> τίκτῃ δ' ἔμπεδα μῆλα, θάλασσα δὲ παρέχῃ ἰχθῦς
> ἐξ εὐηγεσίης, ἀρετῶσι δὲ λαοὶ ὑπ' αὐτοῦ.

> Oh, woman, no one would among mortal men on this endless earth
> reproach you; for indeed your fame reaches broad heaven,

---

[15] All translations are mine, unless otherwise noted.

as that of a <u>blemish-free king</u>,[16] who is god-fearing,
ruling among many and strong men,
who upholds justice, and in return black earth bears
wheat and barley, the trees grow heavy with fruit,
the flock always reproduces, and the sea provides fish,
all from his gentle leadership, and the people prosper under him.[17]

Odyssey 19.107–114

We see that the good king is one who has fame (*kleos*) and whose good leadership (*euēgesiē*) guarantees prosperity (grain, fruit, fish). In the *Odyssey*, such a king is an active ideal, not the reality; it is the exception to the rule, as the various *basileis* reproach and are reproached in turn, do not have *kleos*, are arrogant (*huperphialoi*, *Odyssey* 13.373 and *passim*), and shameless (*anaideisi*, *Odyssey* 13.376). And yet, Telemachus, though the rightful king-to-be, is an inexperienced *nēpios*,[18] thus still unfit for kingship himself. In fact, the only good king in the *Odyssey* is of course Odysseus. Concerning Odysseus' rule, the poetic narrative suggests that he might have ruled too gently (*Odyssey* 2.230–231) and that the suitors failed to properly appreciate his kind and moderate rule (*Odyssey* 2.234). On the other hand, the narrative also points out that Odysseus as a leader was not able to protect his men during the return journey (*Odyssey* 1.1–7). It is clear that he has a few shortcomings.

Thus, in Homeric poetry we find the concepts of the good and bad king within the frame of *appréciation qualifiante*, with stress on competition for the kingship and on reproachful language. The suitors' discourse is by definition contentious and abusive, provoking likewise contentious responses from others. Telemachus, Penelope, Eumaeus, Eurycleia, and Odysseus in his disguise all will reproach the suitors in turn, invariably pointing to their oppressive arrogance, greed, gluttony, and breach of hospitality. In the passage below, Odysseus, disguised as a beggar, tells Antinous that he should be especially generous, precisely because he is a king:

δός, φίλος· οὐ μέν μοι δοκέεις ὁ κάκιστος Ἀχαιῶν
ἔμμεναι, ἀλλ' ὤριστος, ἐπεὶ <u>βασιλῆϊ</u> ἔοικας.
τῷ σε χρὴ δόμεναι καὶ λώϊον ἠέ περ ἄλλοι
σίτου· ἐγὼ δέ κέ σε κλείω κατ' ἀπείρονα γαῖαν.

---

16 I translate *amumōn* as "blemish-free," in conformity with my argument, though most translators render it as the attribute "blameless." For an analysis of the word, see Parry 1973:29–38.

17 Translations of the *Odyssey* are adapted from Samuel Butler (1900) and A.T. Murray (1995).

18 I will discuss the meaning and significance of this word in detail in Chapter 2, section 3.

Give, friend, you do not seem to be the worst among the Achaeans,
rather the best, since you look like a <u>basileus</u>.
You should give an even more generous portion of food
than the others; and I will sing your fame over the boundless earth.

Odyssey 17.415–418

Odysseus sets up a direct connection between benevolent kingship and the provision of food. The king who gives will receive fame through praise, and contrariwise, the ungenerous king must receive blame and blemish as the noble suitors (*mnēstēres-basileis*) will. Thus, criticism attaches to the suitors for their arrogance and lack of generosity until they meet their fate, conceived as an expunging of wrongdoing from the palace. They are slaughtered like animals, but not before sufficient malediction has been invoked against them.

In the Irish epic-mythological cycle, *The Second Battle of Moytura*, a famous satire is made against Bres, king of the Tuatha Dé Danann ("people of the goddess Danu") for his lack of generosity and hospitality toward the poet Cairpre.[19] From that moment on everything went wrong for Bres:

Now the poet Cairpre Mac Edaine came seeking hospitality from his [King Bres's] dwelling. He was conveyed into a small outlying house, which was narrow, dark, and dim, and there was neither fire nor bath nor bed. Three small cakes -- and they [were] dry were brought to him on a little dish. On the next day, he arose, and he was not pleased. As he went out across the court, Cairpre said: "Without food speedily on a platter, without a cow's milk whereon a calf thrives, without a man's habitation after the staying of darkness, be that the luck of Bres Mac Eladain. [May there] not exist now Bres's wealth."

The power of magic in the poet's words destroyed Bres, and he lost everything, just as the power of public reproach (*mōmos*) destroys the suitors. Bres is eventually killed, after being tricked into drinking poisonous waste from cows made of wood. Dumézil interprets this part of the Irish myth as an inversion (*contrepartie*) of the Indian tradition about King Pṛthu, the benevolent king who can provide for his people with a magical and endless abundance of milk from the sacred cow (*la Vache d'Abondance*; *kāmaduh*, or *kamadhenu* in Sanskrit).[20] Thus,

---

[19] Hull 1930. This is referred to as the "first" satire made in Ireland: see Stokes 1891:52–130. See Gray 1982:9; see also Fraser 1916: 103 for *The First Battle of Moytura*.

[20] Dumézil 1943:104–106, and 239. Dumézil's other source is *The Puranas* for which, see Griffith 1895 *Atharva-Veda* 8.10. 24; Tagare, G.V. 1983, 2000: lxxiv; Wilson, 1840: 530. See also Bailey 2003.

abundance in food is conceived at once as a symbol of royal benevolence and as a danger. These contradictory aspects are also present among Penelope's suitors, the *basileis* who *will* eat themselves to death (*Odyssey* 2.237–238) from the abundant wealth (*Odyssey* 1.232) of a "gentle king" (*Odyssey* 2.234).

In Cormaic's glossary (*Sanas Cormaic*) we see the story of Néide mac Adnai present the relationship between a king, refusal, and satire. The satire is made against Gaire (also Caier), king of Connaught[21] by his nephew and adopted son, Néide.[22] This satire had been plotted and orchestrated by Gaire's wife because she loved Néide: *Nin. ol in ben, denasu <u>aoir</u> do coraib <u>ainim</u> fair* (" 'Not difficult,' said the woman. 'Make thou a <u>satire</u> [*aoir* = *áer*] on him so that a <u>blemish</u> [*ainim*] come upon him.' "). Indeed, the satire was illegitimate because it was unjust; Gaire was not miserly. At first Néide feared that Gaire was beyond the reach of satire since the king would not refuse him (Néide) anything.[23] However, when Gaire refused to give Néide his dagger because of an old prohibition, Néide made a satire (*áer*) against him:

> Issi so ind áer:
> "Maile baire gaire Caieur
> combeodutar celtra catha Caier
> Caier dibá Caier dira foró
> fomara fochara Caier."

> This is the satire [*áer*]:
> "Evil [*maile*], death [*baire*], short life [*gaire*] to Caier
> May spears of battle [*celtra catha*] wound Caier!
> Destruction [*dira*] to Caier
> Caier under earth [*foró*]
> Under ramparts [*fomara*], under stones [*fochora*]"

In plotting for the suitors' "last meal," that is, the fattening before the kill (*Odyssey* 20.119, 21.428–430), I see an inversion similar to the mythopoetic idiom *Kamadhenu* (cow of plenty), Dumezil's *Vache d'Abondance*. The suitors too will die from, and in, abundance.

[21] Stokes 1868. See gloss for Gaire (pp. xxxvi–xxxvii): "*Gaire*, that is, *gair-seclae*, that is, *gair-ré*, that is, *régair* ("a short space" [of lifetime]), *ut est* [as is] in the satire which Néide, son of *Adnai*, son of *Guthár*, made on the king of *Connaught*."

[22] Stokes 1868:xxxiv. Néide's name means envy (*neid*); compare *Néit* ("god of battle") and in cognate with Greek *o-neid-os* ("reproach").

[23] While refusing to give a gift could be in itself a flaw incompatible with a good king, it is critical to understand that the legitimacy of the satire, whether justly or unjustly made, must be assessed alongside the nature of the original request, whether just or unjust. In Néide's case, his death stems from the unjust nature of his request.

Following Néide's satire, blisters appeared on Gaire's face: *dobert a laimh dara einech. fogeib teora <u>boulga</u> for a agaidh dosgene ind <u>aor</u>*, "He put his hand over his face. He found on his face three <u>blisters</u> [*boulga*] which the <u>satire</u> [*aér*] had caused."[24] Although the word for "blister" is *boulgae*, Gaire's wife uses the word *ainim*, which according to Breatnach's study on collective abstract nouns in old and early medieval Irish denotes both the blemish and the individual blemished.[25] In addition, *Sanas Cormaic* presents us with the following entry, which includes two original Irish meanings of the word *ferb* (a borrowing from Latin *verbum*):[26]

> Ferb .i. tréde fordingair .i. ferb bó cétamus. *ut est* isint
> [Sh]enchas már. teora ferba fíra .i. tri ba [finda]. Ferb din
> .i. bólc docuirither foraigid duine iarnáir [= "after a satire"] no
>   iarngúbreth.
> *ut est* geal fir natferba forbertatar forainchaib iarom.
> Ferb din .i. briathar. *ut est* rofeass itfás infenechas icondelghree thi
>   ferb ndé.

> *Ferb*, it means three different things, i.e. a 'cow' (*ferb*) in the first place : *ut est* [as it is] in *Senchas Mór* i.e. three white cows (*teora ferba fíra*); *Ferb*, 'also a blotch which is put on the face of a man after a satire or after a false judgment', *ut est* [as it is] in 'the brightness of a man on whose face blotches have not grown afterwards' (*gel fir nat ferba forbertatar for a inchaib iarom*)]. *Ferb* also i.e. a 'word', *ut est* [as is]: 'It is known that the *Fenechas* is void in comparison with the words of God' (*rofeass itfás infenechas icondelghree thi ferb ndé.*)[27]

In the narrative part of the glossary, the verses of Néide's satire are described as *glam dicend*: "Néide made a *glam dicend* upon him, and three blisters [*bulgae*] came forth on his cheeks"(*Dogni neide glam dicend do co toralae teorae bulgae for a gruaidibh*). Dumézil's translation of *glam dicend* as "couplets décochés" (236) offers an image of the poet as an archer shooting his injurious

---

[24] Stokes 1862:xxxviii. *Aor* is the genitive form of *áer*.
[25] Breatnach 2016:6n20
[26] eDIL s.v. *ferb* (eDIL 2019: *An Electronic Dictionary of the Irish Language*, based on the *Contributions to a Dictionary of the Irish Language* (Dublin: Royal Irish Academy, 1913-1976, www.dil.ie 2019).
[27] I thank Elizabeth Gipson for the following comment on the glossary entry for *ferb*: "It is possible that the redactor is pairing the native concept of *áer* (satire) with the native result of *ferb* (blister). One should not conclude from this that the words are interchangeable, or that *ferb* is acting as a replacement for *áer*."

arrows—" 'decocher: envoyer (quelque chose) avec force, lancer (une flèche) avec un arc ou une arbalète, un archer décochant une vole de flèches.' "[28]

Néide's satire[29] caused three blisters to appear on the king's face: stain, blemish, and defect,[30] all of which could be translated by the Greek *mōmos*, as we shall see in a later chapter. Since a blemished king could not rule, Gaire goes into exile, and Néide inherits kingdom and queen.[31] Later, however, riddled by sorrow, Néide goes in search of Gaire. On seeing his adopted son, Gaire dies of shame, and Néide also dies pierced under the eye by a rock, so that the poet who makes an unjust satire injures himself.

> A stone that happened (to be) under Caier's foot
> Sprang up to the height of a
> mast
> It fell—not unjust was the decree—
> On the head of the poet (*filead*)[32]

---

[28] For the notion of the power of poets to injure, see Horace *Satire* 1.4.78: *laedere gaudes*, "you [Horace] love to give pain." Compare Horace's *Satire* 1.4.3-5 for the idea of figuratively "marking" or "branding" someone (*notabant*) through satire: *si quis erat dignus describi, quod malus ac fur / ... multa cum libertate notabant*, "If anyone was worthy of *being described* [in such a way], because he was wicked and a thief ... / they [writers of old comedy] with ample liberty branded him." For the force of the verb *noto*, compare the Greek στίγματα στίζειν, "to brand one with a mark." Horatian satire, though steeped in literary sophistication, is related to both comedy and iambic poetry by tradition. *Satire* 2.3.11–12: *quorsum pertinuit stipare Platona Menandro? / Eupolin, Archilochum, comites educere tantos?* " why did you bother to pack Plato and Menander / and why did you bother to bring along Eupolis, and Archilochus, such great companions."

[29] For Néide as a poet, see *Immacallam in dá Thuarad* in Stokes (1905: 4-64). Russell (2008:23) explains that "those familiar with that text [*Immacallam in dá Thuarad*] would have understood from the beginning of *Gaire* that Néide was a trained poet. This would explain why he could resort to satire." For the magical force of words and the distinction between a curse (*maldacht*, borrowed from Latin) and satire (*áer*), see Cathasaigh 1986:1–15, where St. Patrick's imprecation is a curse (*maldacht*) whereas for Cairpre, the poet, it is satire (*áer*). I thank Joseph Nagy and Elizabeth Gipson for bringing these articles to my attention. For further discussions about satire as the domain of poets and poetry, see Breatnach 2004.

[30] For these specific kinds of blisters, see the story "Wooing of Luaine and the Death of Athirne" (Stokes 1868:270-285): "The damsel [wife of Conchobar] refused to lie with them [Athirne and his two sons Cuindgedach and Apartach]. So, then they made three satires about her, which left three blotches on her cheeks, to wit, Shame and Blemish and Disgrace, black and red and white." These colors were the same as those caused by "unjust satires" (p. 279, note 3).

[31] In the Irish epic-mythological cycle *Cath Maige Tuired, the Battle of Magh Tuireadh* (also *Mag Turead*), King Nuada of the Dé Danann ("people of the goddess Danu"), the invading force from the north, loses his hand in combat with the Fir Bolg ("natives"). The goddess Brigid had ordered that no "blemished" king should rule the Tuatha Dé Danann, so that Nuada is forced to leave the kingship and is succeeded by Bres.

[32] Russell 2008:9–45 suggests that Néide does not die, but is instead blemished in the same way as Gaire, which would make him unfit for kingship. Compare Hipponax frr. 5–10 W and 115 W for the dual role of the blame poet in the construction of the scapegoat, known as *pharmakos*,

1.2 Ancient Scholarship:
Aristotle on Blame Poetry and the *Margites*

Ancient Greek scholarship on praise and blame goes back to Aristotle's general formulations on mimetic arts. He observed that these arts (poetry, drama, epic) operate on the same principles (objects, media, mode), but that they differ in the characters they represent. Moreover, the distinction between praise poetry (*ep-ainos*: hymns and encomia) and blame poetry (*psogos:* iambic poetry)[33] stems from early poetry dividing itself into two different branches, according to the nature of the characters each depicts (*Poetics* 1448b24–27),[34] either noble (*spoudaios*) or base (*phaulos*) (*Poetics* 1448a1). For Aristotle, the poetic descendants of these early branches of poetry were epic and iambic respectively, and from these, tragedy and comedy. However, epic poetry presents a third aspect of speech-making performance or speech acts,[35] besides praise (*kleos*), and blame (*mōmos, oneidos*), namely "admonition" (*ainos*).

Although *ainos*, as an expression of admonition and cautionary tale, may not be applicable to epic as a general designation, its capacity to express blame as well as praise, albeit indirectly, can be discerned in individual speeches in Homer. The "instructive" aspect of *ainos* represented through fable and myth is a rhetorical strategy some of the suitors use in their admonition against Odysseus as a beggar (*Odyssey* 21.295–304). It may be helpful to think of Greek *ainos* in terms similar to what Dumézil outlined as the nature of blame, namely a myth that aims at "establishing its lesson indirectly" (*visant à établir sa leçon indirectement*). What constitutes rightfulness is presented (or learned) in reverse. Thus, the tension between praise and blame can be conceived as direct and indirect modes of discourse. The description of *ainos* as a "double edge" (Nagy 1994:149) mode of discourse fits the situation of the suitors well, in their double role as malevolent kings deserving of blame and as satirists blaming the rightful king.

---

of which I will speak more later on. On the one hand, the poet is the abuser, who constructs a *pharmakos* image of his victims, but on the other, he is the victim himself, paying for his abuses; see Compton 2006.

[33] *Psogos* (*psegō*): a blamable fault, a blemish, flaw (LSJ). I will look more closely at blemishes as the physical aspect of blame in Chapter 4.

[34] In Diodorus Siculus' description of Irish bards, the contrasting pair is *humnoisin* and *blasphēmousi*: εἰσὶ δὲ παρ' αὐτοῖς καὶ ποιηταὶ μελῶν, οὓς βάρδους ὀνομάζουσιν. οὗτοι δὲ μετ' ὀργάνων ταῖς λύραις ὁμοίων ᾄδοντες οὓς μὲν ὑμνοῦσιν, οὓς δὲ βλασφημοῦσι. φιλόσοφοί τέ τινές εἰσι καὶ θεολόγοι περιττῶς τιμώμενοι, οὓς δρουίδας ὀνομάζουσι (5.31.2), "Among them [the Irish] there are poets of songs, whom they call bards. These men, singing with instruments that are like lyres, *praise some*, and *blame others*. There are some who are philosophers, and highly honored theologians, whom they call druids" [my emphasis].

[35] Cf. the concept of Irish *trefocal*, i.e. the three colors of poetry.

Nagy conceives the distinction between *kleos* in praise poetry and in epic poetry in terms of *ainos*, and formulates this distinction in the following way:

> In contrast with the praise poetry of Pindar, the epic poetry of the Homeric *Iliad* and *Odyssey* makes no claims to exclusiveness and does not qualify as a form of *aînos*. Whereas both the epic poetry ... and the praise poetry... qualify as *kléos*, only praise qualifies as *aînos* ... *aînos* can refer to the narrower concept of a speech admonition, or *par-aín-esis* "instructive speech." In addition, it can designate fables, such as those used by Archilochus to admonish his friends or blame his enemies. As a double edge mode of discourse, the *aînos* can admonish or blame as well as praise.[36]

Nagy 1994:149

On the poetic spectrum leading toward scurrility and ridicule, Aristotle compares *psogos* and comedy. Comedy dealt with the "laughable" (*to geloion*), and like *psogos* did not cause pain or destruction, (*Poetics* 1449a32–36). Aristotle names the *Margites* as the starting point of *psogos* poetry in Greek literature: τῶν μὲν οὖν πρὸ Ὁμήρου οὐδενὸς ἔχομεν εἰπεῖν τοιοῦτον ποίημα, εἰκὸς δὲ εἶναι πολλούς, ἀπὸ δὲ Ὁμήρου ἀρξαμένοις ἔστιν, οἷον ἐκείνου ὁ Μαργίτης καὶ τὰ τοιαῦτα, "however, of those [composers of *psogoi*], we are not able to name such poem by anyone before Homer, though likely there were many, but it is possible for us to start from Homer, and his Margites is such a poem, and others like it." (1448b28–30).

Although citing the *Margites* as the Homeric example of *psogos* poetry, Aristotle seems to situate it somewhere in the middle between *psogos* and comedy: οὕτως καὶ τὸ τῆς κωμῳδίας σχῆμα πρῶτος ὑπέδειξεν, οὐ ψόγον ἀλλὰ τὸ γελοῖον, δραματοποιήσας, "so, too he [Homer] was the first who demonstrated the framework of comedy, not by dramatizing *to psogon*, but *to geloion*" (1448b36–37).[37] In his discussion on the nature of wisdom (*sophia*) in the *Nicomachean Ethics*, Aristotle uses the *Margites* as the Homeric illustration for the kind of wisdom that is general, thus not specific to any one skill. It is difficult to surmise from this brief description whether such a characteristic was an especially undesirable thing or simply a laughable matter. The simpleton Margites, described in Plato's *Alcibiades* 2.147b: "πολλὰ" Μαργίτης μὲν "ἠπίστατο ἔργα, κακῶς δέ," φησίν, "ἠπίστατο πάντα," ("'He [Margites] knew many things,' he

---

[36] See n. 21.
[37] My argument, however, is that in the *Odyssey* Homer does dramatize *to psogon*.

said [an unnamed poet], 'but all of them badly' "). In Aristotle, the *Margites* is the Homeric exemplar of blame:

> εἶναι δέ τινας σοφοὺς οἰόμεθα ὅλως οὐ κατὰ μέρος οὐδ' ἄλλο τι σοφούς, ὥσπερ Ὅμηρός φησιν ἐν τῷ Μαργίτῃ "τὸν δ' οὔτ' ἄρ σκαπτῆρα θεοὶ θέσαν οὔτ' ἀροτῆρα οὔτ' ἄλλως τι σοφόν."

> But we think that there are some men who are wise in general terms, but not in any specific area, as Homer says in the *Margites*: "the gods made him wise neither in digging nor in plowing, nor in any other thing."

> Aristotle *Nicomachean Ethics* 6.7.1141

In addition, as part of a dramatization of *to geloion*, the *Margites* is described as impossibly naive in matters of sex:[38]

> Μαργίτης. ἀνὴρ ἐπὶ μωρίᾳ κωμῳδούμενος, ὅν φασιν ἀριθμῆσαι μὲν μὴ πλείω τῶν ε´ δυνηθῆναι· νύμφην δὲ ἀγόμενον μὴ ἅψασθαι αὐτῆς, ἀλλὰ φοβεῖσθαι λέγοντα μὴ τῇ μητρὶ αὐτὸν διαβάλῃ· ἀγνοεῖν δὲ νεανίαν ἤδη γεγενημένον, καὶ πυνθάνεσθαι τῆς μητρὸς εἴγε ἀπὸ τοῦ πατρὸς ἐτέχθη.

> Margites, a man "satirized" for his foolishness, whom they say could not count beyond five; who would not touch his bride when he married, saying that he feared she would slander him to his mother; for he, though already a young man, was ignorant, and wanted to learn from his mother whether he had been born from his father.[39]

> *Suda* 187

The *Margites* might have occupied an intermediary position between *psogos* and *geloion*, as Aristotle remarked, and as such the character of Margites himself may be understood as a representation of *ainos*, as an "admonition" to a friend. Alternatively, the *Margites* could represent an earlier poetic period where all three elements (*psogos*, *geloion*, *ainos*) were less distinct from one another. We seem to be invited to learn a lesson, which could be either serious or irreverent: πόλλ' οἶδ' ἀλωπῆξ, ἀλλ' ἐχῖνος ἓν μέγα, "Many things the fox knows, but

---

[38] There are two entries for the *Margites* in the *Suda*. The passage above refers to entry 187, while entry (a) comes from Aeschines *Against Ctesiphon* 3.160, where Aeschines accuses Demosthenes of having mocked Alexander the Great by calling him a Margites: ἐπωνυμίαν ... Ἀλεξάνδρῳ Μαργίτην ἔθετο [sic], "he gave the nickname Margites to Alexander" (185).

[39] In the last sentence, it is not clear whether Margites did not know whether his father was really his father, or he was such a simpleton that he thought his father might have given birth to him!

the hedgehog, a great one" (Archilochus fr. 201 W). The aphorism is similar to Plato's description of the *Margites* in *Alcibiades 2*.

Notwithstanding the position of the *Margites*, Aristotle's formulation of praise and blame poetry is phrased in terms of subject matter. It does not refer to the status of the character speaking. In other words, praise concerns itself with noble subjects, and blame with the opposite, while characters who are noble in epic can, and often do, engage in blame speeches.[40] The Homeric universe, with its dialogical and speechmaking performances, creates a more fluid system of standards for noble and base characters. Such malleability applies to Thersites in the *Iliad*, whose social status is ambiguous,[41] and to Penelope's suitors, who are nobles (*basileis*): "Antinous, no fair words you speak, though you are noble" (*Odyssey* 17.381). This Homeric inclusiveness admits of a concept of blame discourse whose focus is sometimes not on the status of the speaker but on the style of the speech itself. In this regard, we immediately think of Thersites again, the character who exemplifies poor speechmaking skills.[42]

However, it is important to consider that in the case of Thersites, there is something else at play in his faulty poetic expression. Besides poverty of style and baseness of character, there is also the question of dissent.[43] The narrative itself makes this clear: "While the others *sat down* and remained in their seats / Thersites *alone*, unmeasured in speech, *kept on talking*" (*Iliad* 2.211-212). The contrast between assent and dissent is succinctly expressed by "*sat down*" and "*kept on talking*," whereby we must understand "sitting" as quietly obeying and "talking" as standing up and disrupting. We know that Thersites was standing, as he is making a speech, but this becomes explicit only when Odysseus strikes him with his golden staff (*Iliad* 2.268) and he is forced to *sit down* (*hezeto*).[44] While we can make the case that Thersites' rebellion is based on separation and alienation from the group, the opposite is true for the suitors, who are a band of rebels and

---

[40] Nagy 1979:253-254 analyzes the ways in which Homer diverges from the Aristotelian formulations. Compare Theognis 367-370: "There are many who blame me, base and noble alike."

[41] Elmer 2013:93 asserts that this sense of ambiguity surrounding the social status of Thersites and remarks that those who favor noble lineage do so based on *Iliad* 2.231, where Thersites speaks of taking prisoners, as well as the character's noble lineage outside the *Iliad*. My position on Thersites (Kouklanakis 1999:35-53) favors the general ambiguity that the narrative conveys, but if he should be a *basileus*, even of lower rank, a comparison between him and the suitors, which I intend to make, would be neater.

[42] See Kouklanakis 1999:35-53.

[43] Elmer 2013:96 views Thersites less as a voice of social dissent and more as a disruption to proper political deliberations.

[44] For the representation of dissent as the action of one alone, compare *Odyssey* 10.428-429: "So I spoke and right away they heeded my words / but Eurylochus alone tried to restrain all my comrades."

whose speech is not characterized as faulty but hostile. It is difficult to infer broader sociopolitical trends from the isolated instance of Thersites' rebelliousness, or even from the anomaly of the suitors' behavior (*Odyssey* 18.275), except for what is explicit: Thersites calls for a desertion from battle; the suitors do waste Odysseus' wealth and do plot to ambush and kill Telemachus.[45]

1.3 The View from Pindar: Reproachful Language

Pindar portrays blame poets as "the abusive Archilochus being fattened with heavily worded hatreds:" ψογερὸν Ἀρχίλοχον βαρυλόγοις ἔχθεσιν / πιαινόμενον, (*Pythian* 2.55–56).[46] Pindar emphasizes the figurative gluttony of the offensive poet and refers to his absence of inspiration, and imagination: εἶδον γὰρ ἑκὰς ἐὼν τὰ πόλλ᾽ ἐν ἀμαχανίᾳ, "For I have seen [Archilochus] from afar, often at a loss" (Pindar *Pythian* 2.54). In the poems of iambic poets themselves, we find similar themes of overconsumption, but these are framed in the context of feasting and revelry, as in this Archilochus fragment: ἔωθεν ἕκαστος / ἔπινεν, ἐν δὲ βακχίῃ, "From then on, each man drank in Bacchic style" (fr. 194 W).

Nevertheless, Archilochus also uses the scene of the banquet as an attack against the uninvited and gluttonous guest, as is the case with Pericles below:

> πολλὸν δὲ πίνων καὶ χαλίκρητον μέθυ,
> οὔτε τῖμον εἰσενείκας ⟨ – ˘ – x – ˘ – ⟩
> οὐδὲ μὲν κληθεὶς ⟨ ˘ – x ⟩ ἦλθες οἷα δὴ φίλος,
> ἀλλά σεο γαστὴρ νόον τε καὶ φρένας παρήγαγεν
> εἰς ἀναιδείην,
>
> Drinking much unmixed wine,
> neither do you [Pericles] bring your share ....
> nor invited .... do you come, as a friend unto friends,
> but your belly led astray your mind and good judgment
> into shamelessness.[47]

Archilochus fr. 124b W

---

[45] I will discuss the connection between the suitors' language and iambic poetry, as well as the scapegoat ritual, in more detail in the following chapters.

[46] For the notion of "fattening" as transgression, compare Aeschylus *Agamemnon* 1669: πρᾶσσε, πιαίνου, μιαίνων τὴν δίκην, ἐπεὶ πάρα, "Go on, fatten yourself, polluting justice, as it is your right." Cf. Brown 2006.

[47] Compare Athenaeus *Deipnosophistai* (10.415d): περὶ δὲ Θυὸς τοῦ Παφλαγόνων βασιλέως ὅτι καὶ αὐτὸς ἦν πολυφάγος προειρήκαμεν, "We have before discussed the king of the Paphlagonians, that even he was a glutton."

Whereas Pindar accuses Archilochus of feasting on words of hatred, Archilochus attacks Pericles for feasting on the wine and food of others. Gluttony, fattening, and feasting are thus connected with the greed and envy of those who speak ill and behave badly, as the suitors do.[48] Particularly interesting in view of the Pericles fragment is the notion of a guest who will not contribute his "part" (*timon*) to a banquet. Athena herself remarks this about the suitors (*Odyssey* 1.225–226) and in the absence of their contribution (*eranos*) she observes that they feast as "outrageous" men (*hubrizontes*) and in "arrogant manner" (*huperphialōs*). Telemachus further elaborates on the burden that a guest places on the resources of the host and household. He even offers to support Eumaeus so that the guest (Odysseus) does not become a burden on resources (*Odyssey* 16.83–84). The suitors, for their part, eat and drink from another man's food and wine, though they themselves have plenty in their own houses (*Odyssey* 17.530–537). The suitors represent a perfect conflation of those who fatten themselves both on food and mocking words (*Odyssey* 16.87). To put it another way, they represent the point where the metaphorical and the literal meanings of blame meet.

Blame poetry is conventionally expressed as a foil for praise, or a warning (*ainos*) against wrongdoing or speaking ill.[49] We find in Pindaric poetry, but also in the poems of Bacchylides (5.188, 13.200, 13.202) and Theognis (169),[50] the praise/blame complex conventionally represented in terms of function (foil, admonition), diction (e.g. *psogon* [Pindar *Nemean* 7.61]; *phthoros*, 'pestilent person' [Bacchylides *Dithyrambs* Ode 15.61]), and theme (envy, greed, gluttony, biting criticism, devouring dogs,[51] and shamelessness). The poetic aim of praise poetry is to express its superiority over blame, while the goal of blame poetry is to attack the poet's enemies. In praise poetry we see the juxtaposition between the best and the worst, where the best is the winner himself and the worst is not even a contender, but rather the envious, the one who begrudges, the detractor:

... μῶμος ἐξ ἄλλων κρέμαται φθονεόντων
τοῖς, οἷς ποτε πρώτοις περὶ δωδέκατον δρόμον.

---

[48] An interesting instance of such a connection between insulting and devouring are the words *iambeiophagos*, "devourer of iambs" (i.e. insults), used by Demosthenes against Aeschines (*On the Crown* 18.139), and *iambophagos* (Bekker 1814:190 *Anecdota Graeca* vol. 1). The name Antinous itself (the suitors' ringleader) means "against" or "contrary to sense" (*anti-noos*). It also carries the notion of good judgment led astray by human appetites, particularly gluttony and greed for the kingship.

[49] Compare Pindar *Olympian* 9.1–5, where Archilochus is presented as a poet of praise.

[50] Compare Nagy 1979:223.

[51] For the use of "dog" (*kuōn/kunōpēs*) as an insult in the *Odyssey*, see the following: Melanthius uses 'dog' insults against both Odysseus (as beggar) and Eumaeus (17.248); Odysseus insults the suitors (17.35); and Penelope insults Melantho (19.91–92). Compare *Iliad* 8.379, 11.818. The suitors are like ravenous dogs, eating the hero indirectly by eating the hero's wealth.

blame from other envious men hangs over
those who are ever among the first in the *dōdekaton* race.

Pindar *Olympian* 6.74–75

Further, the superiority of praise relates to the idea that praise is a matter of wisdom, and thus only the wise know how to praise. The idea is expressed in Pindar—ἄνδρα κεῖνον ἐπαινέοντι συνετοί, "that man, wise men praise" (Pindar *Pythian* 5.107)—and again in Bacchylides—φρονέοντι συνετὰ γαρύω, "to the wise I sing what is understandable" (3.85). We can assume that the wise are the nobles dispensing and receiving praise, while the foolish (and offensive) are the base who blame and are blamed in turn.[52] In his "praise of praise" Pindar comes closer to the Indic and Roman poetic modes of appreciation of kings, according to Dumézil's paradigm. Pindar follows the aristocratic bias we see in Aristotle (noble versus base), whereas in Archilochus this duality is disrupted and, in the *Odyssey*, diffused.

1.4 The View from Archilochus: Suitors, Iambic Poetry, and Irish Satire

The suitors' attacks against Telemachus and Odysseus are similar in language and force to iambic poetry and to the iambic sentiment of hostility against enemies (*ekhthroi*) communicated through performance to a company of friends (*hetairoi*).[53] The aggression in the suitors' words reminds us of the violence we find in Archilochus, whose attacks against his *ekhthroi* are direct and unapologetic: ἐν δ' ἐπίσταμαι μέγα / τὸν κακῶς <μ'> ἔρδοντα δεινοῖς ἀνταμείβεσθαι κακοῖς, "But one great thing I know / is to respond viciously to a man who treats me badly" (fr. 126 W).[54] Significantly, the most violent expression in Archilochus' poetry is found in the voice of a slighted suitor attacking his would-be father-in-law, Lycambes, and his would-be bride and her sisters for breaking a personal oath, according to which the poet-suitor would marry his daughter Neoboule:

πάτερ Λυκάμβα, ποῖον ἐφράσω τόδε;
τίς σὰς παρήειρε φρένας
ἧς τὸ πρὶν ἠρήρησθα; νῦν δὲ δὴ πολὺς
ἀστοῖσι φαίνεαι γέλως.

---

[52] Compare Hesiod *Works and Days* 202.
[53] Steinrück 2008:9–17 has proposed an even more direct connection between the suitors and Archilochus. For him, the suitors as a group are identical to Archilochus' audience in generational terms.
[54] Compare Pindar *Pythian* 12.83–84: "to be a *philos* to a *philos* / but [to be] like an *ekhthros* to an *ekhthros*."

Father Lycambes, what were you thinking?
Who has taken away your senses,
which you had before? But now
to the citizens, you are a source of laughter.

Archilochus fr. 172 W

The attack itself reflects the capacity of blame to disqualify and demote. Lycambes, though he may not be a *basileus*, is a prominent citizen, perhaps a tyrant, and Archilochus' poem according to later tradition has the dramatic and fateful effect of driving him to suicide.[55] Indeed, the indignation we hear from Archilochus' mocking voice is similar to Antinous' response to Telemachus in its rhetorical style: "What thing have you said? / Putting us to shame and blaming/blemishing us?" (*Odyssey* 2.85–86). One could see how Telemachus here stands in the place of a future father-in-law (or any other male relative) with the power to obstruct a suitor. In addition, the suitors also see Penelope failing to fulfill her promises, similar to the breaking of the marriage oath in Archilochus. Telemachus is often in the role of Antinous' *ekhthros*, and accordingly the suitor attempts to destroy him in words and with violence.[56] At best, Antinous treats Telemachus as a *hetairos*, who has to deal with their taunting, as I will show in Chapter 2.

The sociolinguistic phenomenon of insulting friends, heaping curses, or speaking indecent things pointedly reminds us of Iambe, the servant woman in the *Homeric Hymn to Demeter* who makes gloomy Demeter smile and laugh with her jests and jokes:[57]

ἀλλ' ἀγέλαστος, ἄπαστος ἐδητύος ἠδὲ ποτῆτος
ἧστο πόθῳ μινύθουσα βαθυζώνοιο θυγατρός,

---

[55] See Bond 1952:10. For the fate of the daughters, see *Greek Anthology* 7.71 (attributed to Gaetulicus), 7.351 (attributed to Dioscorides), 7.352 (attributed to Meleager); Horace *Epodes.* 6.13, *Epistles* 1.19.; Ovid *Ibis* 54 with scholia; Pliny *Natural History* 36.11; Aelian *Various History* 5.8 and scholia.

[56] While actual sexual violence is not expressed in the same way as in Archilochus' attacks on Lycambes and his daughters, Odysseus suggests that, at least in some cases, the suitors slept with Penelope's handmaids (counted as part of the palace's wealth) against their will (*Odyssey* 22.37). Compare *Odyssey* 20.6–8.

[57] In the commentary by Allen and Sikes (1934), the authors say that the connection between Iambe and iambic meter is not correct and that "there is no proof that the Eleusinian raillery was uttered in iambic or any meter" (150). Compare Apollodorus *Library* 1.5.1, where Iambe makes Demeter smile (*meidiasai*), not laugh. In *Odyssey* 20.301–302, the verb *meidiaō* is used to refer to Odysseus' "sardonic smile." Odysseus' smile is a defensive and self-restraining expression against the physical attack from the suitor Ctesippus (*Odyssey* 20.299), and we might assume the same mechanism among dinner *hetairoi* in iambic poetry. Compare Archilochus fr. 171 W. On nonverbal behavior in the Homeric epic, see Lateiner 1998.

πρίν γ' ὅτε δὴ χλεύῃς μιν Ἰάμβη κέδν' εἰδυῖα
πολλὰ παρασκώπτουσ' ἐτρέψατο πότνιαν ἁγνήν,
μειδῆσαι γελάσαι τε καὶ ἵλαον σχεῖν θυμόν·
ἢ δή οἱ καὶ ἔπειτα μεθύστερον εὔαδεν ὀργαῖς.

but not smiling, not eating food, or drinking,
she [Demeter] sat curtailing her longing for her well-girded
daughter,
until trusty Iambe, who knew about jokes,
intervened with jests and made the holy mistress [Demeter],
smile and laugh and feel her heart lighter:
indeed she [Iambe] afterwards continued to delight her mood.

Homeric Hymn to Demeter 200–205

Iambe relieves the goddess from her perennial grief, at least momentarily.[58] In this specific instance the connection between Iambe and the spirit of iambic poetry works well; Demeter's reaction is amused precisely because Iambe's language is likely salacious. It is Demeter's laughter that gives us the clue that Iambe is a friend, *philē*, not a foe, an *ekhthra*.[59]

Nevertheless, despite Telemachus' role as the suitors' competitor for the kingship of Ithaca, it is Odysseus who plays the critical role of *ekhthros*; he is the consummate opponent to the malevolent *basileis* and the ultimate contender for bride and kingship. Odysseus as beggar adds to the hero's "polytropic" ways, and the narrative explores this social inversion whereby king is now both beggar and satirical poet, roles which allow Odysseus to appreciate a host's generosity or depreciate him for his stinginess. The contrast between appreciation and depreciation is analogous to Indic poetry, and Irish satire, respectively. In addition, beggars and poets are often "guest and strangers" (*xenoi*). Disrespect of a beggar can incur punishment from the gods and reproach from the people (*Odyssey* 18.221–225) as harshly as disrespect for the king. Although not wanted or invited (*Odyssey* 17.382–387), the beggar-stranger (*xeinos*) could be a god or a messenger of the gods (*Odyssey* 17.484–487). Thus, Antinous' begrudging of the beggar's presence and the food he partakes heightens the suitors' transgressions because here beggar and king are the same.

---

[58] Compare *Odyssey* 18.174, where Penelope's housekeeper, Eurynome, tells her "it is not good to grieve unceasingly."

[59] In the *Odyssey*, it is also laughter that interrupts grief and lamentation, not by "dirty words," as in Iambe's case, but by Telemachus' sneeze (*Odyssey* 17.541–542). The sneeze is taken as a good omen and gives Penelope temporary relief from her predicament.

The Bold, the Satirist, the *Nēpios*

2.1 Thersites, Suitors, and the Language of Reproach

As the embodiment of blame in the *Iliad*,[1] Thersites is marked by a speech style that is referred to by the narrative and Odysseus himself as poorly conceived and constructed.[2] He is identified by his ugliness in words (*Iliad* 2.213) and in physical appearance (*Iliad* 2.216); he is disagreeable in every way.[3] The suitors, conceived as blame poets or epic satirists, so to speak, are unbecoming in their arrogant behavior and cutting words. The fact that they are young and some of them even handsome, as Odysseus says of Antinous, creates a dissonance between their pleasant appearance and their malicious character, a juxtaposition Odysseus points out: ὦ πόποι, οὐκ ἄρα σοί γ' ἐπὶ εἴδεϊ καὶ φρένες ἦσαν, "alas, your thoughts do not accord to your beauty" (*Odyssey* 17.454).

Nevertheless, the narrative never indicates that their words are disorganized in the way we are told of Thersites, whose unseemliness is conceived as a problem of form, both of his physical body and of his words.[4] The suitors,

---

[1] See Nagy 1979:259–262. This study is critical for the understanding of praise and blame as key generic forces in Greek poetry, and is "pioneering" (Rosen 2003:122) for the view of Thersites as a paradigmatic blame poet that fits within this ancient poetic framework.

[2] In an earlier article "Thersites, Odysseus and Social Order" (Kouklanakis 1999:35–53), I had proposed that Thersites' ambiguous status is reflected in the discrepancy between the narrative's unequivocally negative view of his style (disorderly and verbose) and his actual speech, which tries and sometimes does achieve a certain rhetorical flair (*Iliad* 2.225–242). However, the point here is not so much his actual speech, but his petulance and impertinence framed within a code of blame poetics, namely his misrepresentation of Achilles' wrath, as well as his envy of Agamemnon. Misrepresentation and envy are the definition of blame in Pindar (*Nemean* 8.32–33, *Olympian* 6.73–75).

[3] Compare Smith 1966:554 on the physiological implications for "moral and emotional integrity." Smith is not speaking of Thersites here, but his observation that there is a mirror effect between emotional upset and physiological expressions, such as at *Odyssey* 23.205–207, seems relevant also for the mirrorlike reflection of Thersites' character in his physique.

[4] Thersites' name itself indicates impertinence: *thers-/thars-* from *tharsos* "boldness", understood in negative terms). For further discussion on Thersites and ideology, see Thalmann (1988), for

on the other hand, are unseemly because they are arrogant and shameless, and because they are speakers of reproach. In short, they combine *hubris te biē te*, "both hubris and violence" (*Odyssey* 17.565).[5] The conjunction of *neikos* ("quarrel," "strife") and *aeikēs* ("unseemly") is aptly used to describe the insolent herdsman Melanthius, whose allegiance to the suitors is echoed by his insulting language against Odysseus and Eumaeus: τοὺς δὲ ἰδὼν νείκεσσεν ἔπος τ' ἔφατ' ἔκ τ' ὀνόμαζεν, / ἔκπαγλον καὶ <u>ἀεικές</u>·[6] ὄρινε δὲ κῆρ Ὀδυσῆος, "And when he [Melanthius] saw them [Odysseus led by Eumaeus], he started to abuse them, spoke an *epos*, and addressed them / with violent and *unseemly* words, and he stirred Odysseus' heart" (*Odyssey* 17.215–216).

"Unseemliness" means "that which is not to be seen or done," and thus not right nor beautiful, a connection we clearly see in the contrast between *aeikeiē* "unseemly" and *kala* "beautiful" (*Odyssey* 16.109). After Ctesippus hurls a hoof of ox at Odysseus (*Odyssey* 20. 299-301), Telemachus warns the suitors against "unseemly impropriety": τῷ μή τίς μοι ἀεικείας ἐνὶ οἴκῳ / φαινέτω, "let no one display / make visible unseeming acts in my household" (*Odyssey* 20.308–309).[7] In its extreme expression, *aeikeiē* could lead to *lōbē* ("outrage," "mistreatment," "shame," "insult," and "ruin"). While *aeikeiē* is euphemistic, *lōbē* is a more direct and dark reference to bitter and outlandish insult (*Odyssey* 18.346–348), inde-cent behavior (*Odyssey* 19.373), cause of reproach (*Odyssey* 18.225, 20.169), and mockery (*Odyssey* 23.15, 26). " Telemachus' choice of *aeikeiē* instead of outrage (*lōbē*, *Odyssey* 20.308) may be more strategic in the immediate context; it is more important to guard Odysseus' cloak-and-dagger plan to take revenge against the suitors. Telemachus delays gratification (αἲ γὰρ δή, Εὔμαιε, θεοὶ τισαίατο λώβην, "would that the gods would avenge their insult," *Odyssey* 20.169), just as Odysseus copes with Ctesippus' insult with a sardonic smile (*Odyssey* 20.301–302).

---

close examination of Thersites' language, see Kouklanakis (1999). For an interesting discussion of the double meaning of *tharsos*, see Maiullari 2003.

[5] The expression *hubris te biē te* is often used to describe these young men (*Odyssey* 15.329 and elsewhere).

[6] Compare *Iliad* 22.256: "I will do you no violence" (ἔκπαγλον ἀεικιῶ, *ekpaglon aeikiō*), where violence means that Hector will not do anything that is not ethical within the rules of combat. Compare *Odyssey* 10.448: "he feared my violent reproach" (ἔδεισεν γὰρ ἐμὴν ἔκπαγλον ἐνιπήν, *edeisen gar emēn ekpaglon enipēn*).

[7] *Aeikeiē* ("unseemliness") as a concept in Homer carries ethical, moral, and aesthetic implications. Its poetic form *aeikelios* is sometimes used, and its meaning ranges from "harsh" and "cruel" (*Odyssey* 4.244, 8.231) to "shameless," as in Telemachus' line above (*Odyssey* 16.107, 20.308), to "unsophisticated," "coarse," and "poor" (*Odyssey* 6.242, 19.341), to "physically unattractive" (*Odyssey* 13.402). See *Iliad* 24.19 where Apollo guarded Hector's skin from "injury" (*aeikeiē*). At *Iliad* 24.22, 54 *aeikizein* is used for Achilles' attempt to destroy Hector's dead body. It is instructive to consider the literal sense of *aeikēs*: "what is not habitual," "not like the norm," "strange."

Moreover, the word *lōbē* carries a physical connotation in its meaning as "disfigurement," which, though absent in Homer, is present in Herodotus (*Histories* 3.154). In this connection, *aeikea lōbē* offers fit representation of Thersites, whom the soldiers called *lōbētēr* (*Iliad* 2.275), a reference also to his physical attributes. While Thersites' "unseemliness" as a speaker of abusive words is comparable to the suitors, his function within the narrative is not. Thersites' episode marks the end of any Iliadic laughter of whatever nature— "harmful" (*psogeros*) or "humorous" (*geloios*).[8] Following Thersites' episode, battles will come to dominate the rest of the narrative. Even when we do find harsh words, they do not cause laughter. In contrast to the role of laughter in the *Iliad*, the mocking laughter among the suitors is pervasive and perverse, increasing in intensity until their death (*Odyssey* 20.345–349). Still, despite the difference in the function, scope, and impact of their presence on the overall narrative, both Thersites and the suitors are unheroic[9] characters, and they use the tropes of blame discourse. Such discourse is formalized by diction characterizing reproach and abuse: *mōmos*, "brand," "blame," "blemish" (2.86); *neikos*, "quarrel" (18.9); *eris* "strife" (20.267); *oneidos*, "insults" (17.461, 18.326, 18.380); *lōbe*, "outrage" (2.323, 19.373, 20.169, 20.285); *aiskhea*, "shamelessness" (19.373); *kertomeō*, "abuse" (2.323, 16.87, 18.350, 20.177), *kertomia* (20.263), and *philokertomos* (22.287)—to name several.

The suitors are not returning heroes, nor are they storytellers,[10] thus they are incomplete and unfulfilled, both in terms of epic manhood and in their marital status. Although the suitors are not referred to as *ateleis* (incomplete) directly, the adjective *atelēs* can designate "unmarried person," an obvious attribute of suitors by definition.[11] The positive attribute, *teleios*, is not used to

---

[8] The laughter of the soldiers at Thersites' expense may recall the laughter of the gods at Hephaestus' expense at the end of the first book of the *Iliad* (1.599)—a lame god and a lame mortal. Compare Brown 1989.

[9] Martin 1989:16–18 observes that Thersites does not have a heroic *muthos* because he has no memorable deed to tell.

[10] Odysseus' ability to delight with his stories is an effective source of power. He sings like an *aoidos* who tells his *muthos* knowingly, *epistamenōs* (*Odyssey* 11.368). The beauty of his speech is compared to snowflakes (*Iliad* 3.221–224). His "odyssey," as he tells it to the Phaeacians, allows him to express his identity: "I am Odysseus, son of Laertes, who excels in all manner of strategies" (*Odyssey* 9.19–20). This is his own voice, and he sings the praises of his past adventures up to the present time of Scheria (books 9–11). Odysseus' journey is a brilliant illustration of the hero's deeds, and he has "beauty of words" (*morphē epeōn* [*Odyssey* 11.367]), and "outstanding spirit" (*phrenes esthlai* [*Odyssey* 11.367]). Storytelling is a valued gift exchange in guest-host relations (*xenia*) and reveals Odysseus' excellence in survival strategies, as Muellner 1976:96 has pointed out. Compare Pache 1999:21–33 on guest-host gift exchange.

[11] Compare *Defixionum Tabellae* Audollent 68a. For the connection between the heroic and masculine, the Latin word *vir* (Greek *anēr*) addresses all the categorical roles against which the suitors do not measure up: hero, man, and husband.

designate "married" in Homer, but it refers instead to the wholesomeness of sacrificial victims (*Iliad* 1.66), that is, the condition of being unblemished. The suitors' identities are "unfulfilled" because they are not defined by the battlefield or the trials of exile, nor yet by the difficult responsibilities of being a husband. Rather, they live in the domestic sphere of Penelope's palace (neither wholly private nor public), enjoying banquets, games, feasting, singing, and dancing. But above all, they wait. Their waiting and lingering before Penelope chooses one of them represent a de facto takeover of Odysseus' palace. The lingering and delay also fulfill the narratological need to allow Odysseus time to return. But perhaps, more relevant still is that this waiting is inaction, which highlights the suitors' heroic deficit and indicates that they inhabit the female domestic space and perspective, changed in times of war, when military work abroad (the male space) could be long.[12] The suitors' abusive language stresses this "deficiency" in poetic performance as well, a deficit described by Pindar as a sign of *amakhania* ("helplessness," "lack of skills"):

> ... ἐμὲ δὲ χρεών
> φεύγειν δάκος ἀδινὸν κακαγοριᾶν
> εἶδον γὰρ ἑκὰς ἐὼν τὰ πόλλ᾽ <u>ἐν ἀμαχανίᾳ</u>
> ψογερὸν Ἀρχίλοχον βαρυλόγοις ἔχθεσιν
> πιαινόμενον· τὸ πλουτεῖν δὲ σὺν τύχᾳ πότμου σοφίας ἄριστον.

> As for me, I must
> escape the unrelenting bite of speaking ill.
> for I have seen from afar and often in <u>helplessness/lacking in skills</u>,
> the *psogos* poet Archilochus fattening himself
> with deeply hateful words: but to be rich in destiny
> is the best part of wisdom.

> Pindar *Pythian* 2.52–56

Lack of means or skills (*amakhania*) in poetry is analogous to the meaning of *akosma* ("disorderly") in Thersites' speech and to the suitors' *ateleia* in words and deeds. Furthermore, this notion of flaw and deficiency, the poverty in deeds and words is inscribed in Antinous' own words (*mōmon anapsai*) spoken as a counterattack against Telemachus. The suitors' absence of heroic identity combined with frustration from their unsuccessful wooing leaves them with blame tropes, the dominant mode of discourse to articulate their resentment. Antinous, the most aggressive among them, puts the situation to Telemachus

---

[12] See Aristophanes *Lysistrata* 99–106 for this theme.

forcefully and clearly: they will not quit from their ruinous consumption of Telemachus' (and Odysseus') wealth until Penelope chooses one of them for her husband (*Odyssey* 2.86–128).[13]

Thus, they disregard what is proper in courtship and for the guest-host relationship: they eat and drink too much and do not contribute their part. They therefore break the social contract between guest and host, a critical social context for the dispensation of either praise or blame. Odysseus, on the other hand, is quite aware of the delicate relationship between guests and hosts.[14] Some of the young men in Phaeacia, the would-be suitors of Nausicaa (King Alcinous' daughter), insolently challenge him to enter into an athletic contest with them, though he is unwilling. Odysseus reluctantly accepts the challenge, and even taunts them with his own bragging, but he is wise to spare Laodamas, the son of king Alcinous, his host, thus avoiding blame:

πάντων Φαιήκων, πλήν γ' αὐτοῦ Λαοδάμαντος.
ξεῖνος γάρ μοι ὅδ' ἐστί· τίς ἂν φιλέοντι μάχοιτο;
ἄφρων δὴ κεῖνός γε καὶ οὐτιδανὸς πέλει ἀνήρ,
ὅς τις ξεινοδόκῳ ἔριδα προφέρηται ἀέθλων
δήμῳ ἐν ἀλλοδαπῷ· ἕο δ' αὐτοῦ πάντα κολούει.

Of all the Phaeacians, except Laodamas himself.
For he is my host, and who would quarrel with one showing
    friendship?
Foolish is that man, at any rate worth nothing,
who brings forth competitive strife
to his host among a strange people; indeed, he diminishes all that
    is his.

Odyssey 8.207–211.

Antinous is especially guilty of breaching codified guest-host relations, because his father had once been helped by Odysseus (*Odyssey* 16.424–430).[15] It is because of this familial relationship that Penelope appeals to him to treat kindly the

---

[13] This warning is echoed by Eurymachus (*Odyssey* 2.203–205). The suitors' consumption of animals, oxen, sheep, and pigs represents an inversion of what suitors are expected to do, that is, to enrich the woman for whom they are competing. Compare *Iliad* 18.593, where brides are described as *parthenoi alphesiboiai* (young women priced at many cattle).

[14] Pindar *Nemean* 7.61–63 reminds us that a guest-stranger (*xeinos*) should keep away from dark blame (*skoteinon psogon*). The host too has obligations towards his guest: to house and feed him, to clothe him, and to give supplies and gifts, including women.

[15] Compare *Iliad* 6.120–236, where Glaucus and Diomedes recognize each other, and Diomedes recalls the ties of hospitality that bound their fathers and hence them to each other (*Iliad* 6.215).

stranger (Odysseus as beggar) and honor the friendship (*philotēs*) his own family once enjoyed from the Laertidae.[16] Antinous, however, disregards such bonds, and Penelope calls him *margos*, a term that simultaneously describes his madness, pugnaciousness, greed, and gluttony.[17] This conflation of these three characteristics is neatly articulated in a fragment from Ibycus (fr. 311(a) PMG): Ἔριδός ποτε μάργον ἔχων στόμα, "having the gluttonous-mad mouth of Eris,"[18] so that in the personification of *eris* ("conflict"), the mouth is for quarreling and for overeating.

Finally, insofar as I have been making an explicit comparison between Thersites and the suitors as Homeric examples of blame poets or epic satirists, gluttony offers a distinction: the suitors are described as gluttonous, while Thersites is not. Yet, when Odysseus warns Thersites "not to dare to speak of kings," that is, not to quarrel with them, he uses the idiomatic expression "to hold someone in one's mouth," that is, to insult them and quarrel. The word "mouth" (*stoma*), as in the Ibycus fragment above, juxtaposes the language of quarrel and reproach with the image of the voracious mouth.[19]

> τῷ οὐκ ἂν βασιλῆας ἀνὰ στόμ' ἔχων ἀγορεύοις,
> καί σφιν ὀνείδεά τε προφέροις, νόστόν τε φυλάσσοις.
> οὐδέ τί πω σάφα ἴδμεν ὅπως ἔσται τάδε ἔργα,
> ἢ εὖ ἦε κακῶς νοστήσομεν υἷες Ἀχαιῶν.
> τῷ νῦν Ἀτρείδῃ Ἀγαμέμνονι ποιμένι λαῶν
> ἧσαι ὀνειδίζων, ὅτι οἱ μάλα πολλὰ διδοῦσιν
> ἥρωες Δαναοί· σὺ δὲ κερτομέων ἀγορεύεις.

> Then, do not attempt to speak, devouring kings with your mouth
> And to cast forth insults, looking out for our return.
> In no way do we clearly know how these deeds will come to pass,
> whether well or badly we will return, the sons of the Achaeans.
> And now against Agamemnon, the son of Atreus, shepherd of the
>   people,

---

[16] The story of Heracles' killing of Iphitus (*Odyssey* 21.25–30) is the more outrageous because Iphitus was his guest.

[17] Moreover, the gluttony of the suitors leads to the diminished wealth of Penelope's palace.

[18] Based on this and on other passages, mostly from Pindar, Nagy 1979:230–231 observes that the public beggar Irus fits with the traditional designation of blame poets. Compare *Odyssey* 18.2, where the public beggar Irus is described as having a greedy belly (*gasteri margēi*). The word *margos* is of course also related to *Margites*.

[19] For a study on abuse and on how it is centered on the mouth, see Worman 2008.

you sit[20] there, hurling abuses, because of the many gifts the
Danaan heroes give to him: yet you go on speaking in mockery.

Iliad 2.250–256

The literal translation of βασιλῆας ἀνὰ στόμ' ἔχων is "having or holding kings up in your mouth," that is, bad-mouthing, criticizing, reproaching, and abusing kings, but I chose to translate *ekhōn* ("having") as "devouring" for both its literal ("eating") and figurative ("destroying") meanings. In other words, *ekhōn* (having) means eating and consuming food (as it does in English). Likewise, consumption and destruction characterize the suitors as devourers (*edontes*). Thus, gluttony is also inferred in Thersites' behavior, even if indirectly through his greed and envy, the same two vices Odysseus ascribes to Thersites (*Iliad* 2.256) and the suitors in the *Odyssey*. But unlike Thersites, Penelope's suitors, notwithstanding their arrogance and wrong-doing, do manage to raise the specter of criticism over Odysseus' fate and over his rightful status as king. [21]

---

[20] For another instance of "sitting" as an aggressive stance, rather than obedience, see Chapter 3, Section 2 (the case with the suitors). Sitting in judgement (finding fault, criticizing, casting reproaches) is what judges do, οἱ καθήμενοι, "the seated" (Thucydides 5. 85; Demosthenes 6.3). In this connection it is interesting to consider the stories connected with Momus ("Criticism," "Mockery," "Reproach"), one of Night's children (Hesiod *Theogony* 214). He appears as a judge (*dikastēs*) criticizing the man Hephaestus made because a little door had not been left in the man's breast so that one could look into his [=the man's] secret thoughts (Lucian *Hermotimus* 20). According to Momus, Aphrodite alone was blameless (Philostratus *Epistolae* 21). In the scholiast to *Iliad* 1.5 (fr. 1 W) Momus appears as Zeus' adviser: "For they say that Earth, being weighed down by the multitude of people, there being no piety among humankind, asked Zeus to be relieved from the burden. Zeus firstly and at once brought about the Theban War, by means of which he destroyed large numbers, and afterwards the Trojan one, with Cavil [Momos] as his adviser, this being what Homer calls the plan of Zeus, seeing that he was capable of destroying everyone with thunderbolts or floods. Cavil prevented this, and proposed two ideas to him, the marrying of Thetis to a mortal and the birth of a beautiful daughter. From those two events war came about between Greeks and barbarians, resulting in the lightening of Earth as many were killed. . ." (Translation by M.L. West). If we were to "re-personify" Momus in the phrase *mōmon anapsai*, then Antinous is telling Telemachus not to sit in judgment. Antinous rejects Telemachus' capacity to rule (as the rightful inheritor of kingship), and to settle the affairs in the palace. Yet, the role of Greek kings (*basileis*) included a judicial function in the settling of disputes.

[21] I refer to the apologetic gestures that Odysseus and the *Odyssey* make for the loss of his companions (*Odyssey* 1.5–10). The slaughter of the suitors (though of a different nature) offers a parallel to the loss of Odysseus' companions (*Odyssey* 24.426) insofar as it compromises the hero's reputation.

2.2 Suitors, Makers of Satire

In the first books of the *Odyssey*, Telemachus is the main victim of the suitors' attacks, following his condemnation of the young men at the assembly (*Odyssey* 2.40–79). For the suitors, Telemachus represents the male relative denying them a path to marriage. Yet, since the suitors are also courting the kingship of Ithaca, Telemachus is the king they seek to disqualify through insult, ambush, and death. At *Odyssey* 1.386 and 22.51–53, Telemachus' kingship, which seems to be up for grabs, as Telemachus himself acknowledges (*Odyssey* 1.394–396), is brought up as the very thing the suitors are competing for.[22] Thus, Telemachus is vulnerable to criticism, especially at this point in the narrative. When stirred by Athena, Telemachus begins to claim his position in the palace and to see himself as king, or at least as "master" (*anax*) of his house (*Odyssey* 1.397–398).[23]

Telemachus' role as antagonist to the suitors also turns him into a blame poet, whose purpose is to paint a picture of these young *basileis* as incompatible with their pursuit of Penelope and of the kingship of Ithaca. First, they behave poorly (*Odyssey* 2.48–49): they do not properly woo Penelope, do not send gifts to her father, and do not retreat to their own homes (*Odyssey* 2.52–54). Second, they lay waste to the palace with constant feasts (*Odyssey* 2.55–58). These charges are meant to publicly reproach them, to "blemish them" (*mōmon anapsai*), but Telemachus does this indirectly, by addressing the Achaean citizens with admonitions against their complacency toward the suitors' egregious behavior:

> ... νεμεσσήθητε καὶ αὐτοί,
> ἄλλους τ'αἰδέσθητε περικτίονας ἀνθρώπους,
> οἳ περιναιετάουσι· θεῶν δ' ὑποδείσατε μῆνιν,
> μή τι μεταστρέψωσιν ἀγασσάμενοι κακὰ ἔργα.
>
> You should be ashamed yourselves,
> and feel shame also before your neighbors,
> who live around you: and fear the wrath of the gods.
> lest they turn against you, angered at your evil deeds.
>
> *Odyssey* 2.64–67

---

[22] Compare Thersites' words with Odysseus' characterization of Thersites' verbal attack against Agamemnon (*Iliad* 2.211–277). Thersites is the one who was always abusing, (oneidizon [*Iliad* 2.255]) and quarreling, (erizemenai [*Iliad* 2.214]) with kings. Likewise, Antinous is described as having the habit of speaking harshly (*Odyssey* 17.394).

[23] Telemachus is called a "hero" once at *Odyssey* 4.303: Τηλέμαχός θ' ἥρως καὶ Νέστορος ἀγλαὸς υἱός, "Telemachus, the hero and the brilliant son of Nestor."

Nevertheless, despite Telemachus' harsh words, Antinous rebukes him and points instead to the young man's own flaws. Antinous' words often refer to Telemachus' own unsuitability for the kingship despite his birthright (*Odyssey* 1.387).[24] He mocks the young man's "fancy talk" and "bold words" (*Odyssey* 1.385) as an ironic way to emphasize that Telemachus is either not a good speaker (*Odyssey* 1.384) or that his words do not matter.[25] Antinous believes that, since men did not teach Telemachus to be a fancy talker (*hupsagorēn emenai*) and to speak boldly (*tharsaleōs*), he must have been taught by a god (*Odyssey* 1.385).[26] Indeed, as satirists, the suitors perform their disapproval and derision of Telemachus whenever he speaks:

> ὣς ἔφαθ', οἱ δ' ἄρα πάντες <u>ὀδὰξ ἐν χείλεσι φύντες</u>
> Τηλέμαχον θαύμαζον, ὃ θαρσαλέως ἀγόρευε.

> Thus, he spoke, and they were all <u>biting their lips</u>,
> They were amazed at Telemachus, that he spoke so boldly.

> *Odyssey* 1.381–382

Eustathius's commentary on this passage, and on the expression "biting their lips," states the following:

> διὸ καὶ Ἀντίνοος ὑψαγόρην αὐτὸν ἐρεῖ, τουτέστι πιθανολόγον, μεγαλορρήμονα, τὰ μικρὰ καὶ ταπεινὰ ὑψηλῶς ἀγορεύοντα. Ἔνθα σημείωσαι ὅτι τε τὸ ὀδὰξ ἐν χείλεσι φύντες παλαιός τις ὀδὰξ ἐνδεδηχότες γράφει καὶ ὅτι τὸ | ὑψαγόρης, εἰ καὶ τὸν μεγαληγόρον σημαίνει καὶ δεινὸν εἰπεῖν, ὅμως οὐκ ἂν ἐπὶ ἐπαίνου ὀρθῶς ῥηθείη πρός τινος· δηλοῖ γὰρ μᾶλλον τὸν ψεύστην καὶ συκοφάντην, σχηματισθὲν εὐφημότερον καὶ σεμνότερον Ἰστέον δὲ ὅτι ἐπὶ ἀπτοήτου καὶ φοβεροῦ δημηγόρου καλὸν εἰπεῖν τὸ οἳ δ' ἄρα πάντες ὀδὰξ ἐν χείλεσι φύντες ἐθαύμαζον ὃ

---

[24] Compare *Odyssey* 15.533, where Odysseus (as a beggar) describes Telemachus as the most suitable for kingship precisely by virtue of descent: ὑμετέρου δ' οὐκ ἔστι γένεος βασιλεύτερον ἄλλο, "there is no other kind more royal than you".

[25] Antinous' criticism is inappropriate from the point of view of the epic's bias precisely towards loftiness of style. Antinous understands this bias because his criticisms are often indirect and sarcastic. In this regard then, the suitors, like Callimachus' *Mōmos* and *Phthonos* in the *Hymn to Apollo* (105-113), are incapable of understanding proper style. For Callimachus, less is more, for the epic, praise, not blame, is monumental. Compare Pindar *Olympian* 6.74-75 for the connection between *mōmos* and *phthonos*: ... μῶμος ἐξ ἄλλων κρέμαται φθονεόντων / τοῖς, οἷς ποτε πρώτοις περὶ δωδέκατον δρόμον, "reproach from the envious hangs / over those who are ever among the first in the *dōdekaton* race"; see Kohnken 1981.

[26] Eustathius *Commentaries on Homer's Odyssey* at 1.384-387 (Cullhed 2006:309). The comment that Telemachus was not taught how to speak well by mortal men focuses our attention on Telemachus growing up without a father, the one who would have taught him.

θαρσαλέως ἀγόρευε. Σημείωσαι δὲ καὶ ὅτι καὶ θυμοῦ πολλάκις ἔνδειξις τὸ ὀδὰξ ἐν χείλεσι φῦναι, ὡς δηλοῖ καὶ ὁ Κωμικὸς ἐν Ἀχαρνεῦσιν εἰπών· ὑπ᾽ ὀργῆς τὴν χελύνην ἐσθίων, ὅ ἐστι δάκνων σφιγκτῶς τὸ χεῖλος. ἔστι δὲ ὀδὰξ τὸ δηκτικῶς καὶ μετὰ δαγμοῦ, ὡς προείρηται.

For this reason [Telemachus' indignant speech at the assembly] Antinous calls him *hypsagorēs*, meaning "persuasive speaker", "big-worded", one who speaks sublimely about small and simple things. Note here that one of the ancients wrote "biting with their teeth" instead of "gripping their lips with their teeth", and also that | *hypsagorēs*, even if it signifies a person who is big-worded and forceful in speaking, would be used incorrectly about someone if the aim is to praise him. For it denotes rather a liar and a sycophant, used as a figure of speech in a euphemistic and solemn manner. One must know that when referring to an undaunted and frightening public speaker it is good to say "gripping the lips with their teeth all were astonished at what he courageously said." Note also that the act of gripping the lips with the teeth often signifies anger, as the Comedian shows in Acharnians, saying: "eating his lip with fury", meaning "biting the lip tightly". The word *odax* means "bitingly" and "with a bite", as previously stated.[27]

Antinous's intention is to mock Telemachus' ignorance with sarcastic comments about the young man's highfalutin words (Eustathius v. 383-387). Indeed, the facial expression conveyed by "biting the lips" seems to indicate more reasonably bitterness and anger rather than "amazement." The suitors disdain Telemachus' speech and are sarcastic, precisely in the meaning of the Greek verb *sarkazō*, "to tear flesh like dogs" (LSJ) as we see in Aristophanes' *Pax* 482.[28] The image of tearing flesh is itself used in blame poetry to represent envy, greed, and abusive language, as I have been discussing.[29] Antinous goes on with his sarcasm and curses Telemachus with an imprecation (*eparatai legōn*), not unlike Irish satire:

> Τηλέμαχ᾽, ἦ μάλα δή σε διδάσκουσιν θεοὶ αὐτοὶ
> ὑψαγόρην τ᾽ ἔμεναι καὶ θαρσαλέως ἀγορεύειν·
> μὴ σέ γ᾽ ἐν ἀμφιάλῳ Ἰθάκῃ βασιλῆα Κρονίων
> ποιήσειεν, ὅ τοι γενεῇ πατρώιόν ἐστιν.

---

[27] Translation by Cullhed 2006:309.

[28] Albeit from a later period, we find *sarkazō* (biting the lips) in Galen 19.136 as a symptom of rage.

[29] Compare the meaning of *sarkazō* in Galen 19.136: "to bite the lips in rage, hence "to speak bitterly," "to sneer," (LSJ), which again reflects more closely the suitors' true sentiment. The adjective *thaumazon*, "they were amazed," coupled with "biting their lips" (*Odyssey* 1.381–382) is meant to be ironic.

Telemachus, truthfully, the gods themselves are teaching you
to be a fancy talker and to speak boldly.
May the son of Cronus not crown you king of sea-girted Ithaca,
which is your right by birth.

Odyssey 1.384–387

In addition, Antinous reacts against what he considers Telemachus' fool-ishness, because he (Telemachus) allows the trusted swineherd Eumaeus to invite a beggar (Odysseus) to his halls. Antinous quarrels with Eumaeus as an indirect insult to Telemachus. Antinous ironically complains about the beggar consuming the food of the palace, as though he were the host:

ὣς ἔφατ', Ἀντίνοος δ' ἔπεσιν νείκεσσε συβώτην·
"ὦ ἀρίγνωτε συβῶτα, τίη δὲ σὺ τόνδε πόλινδε
ἤγαγες; ἦ οὐχ ἅλις ἧμιν ἀλήμονές εἰσι καὶ ἄλλοι,
πτωχοὶ ἀνιηροί, δαιτῶν ἀπολυμαντῆρες;
ἦ ὄνοσαι ὅτι τοι <u>βίοτον κατέδουσιν ἄνακτος</u>
ἐνθάδ' ἀγειρόμενοι, σὺ δὲ καὶ προτὶ τόνδ' ἐκάλεσσας;"

Thus, he spoke, and Antinous rebuked the swineherd with [harsh]
    words:
"Oh, famous swineherd, why have you brought this man
from the city? Do we not have enough wanderers and
other troublesome beggars, spoilers of feasts?
Or do you scorn that <u>they devour the livelihood of your master</u>,
gathering here, that you have called also this one?"

Odyssey 17.374–379

Telemachus understands that the challenge is meant for him. The idea of begrudging food is itself encoded in Antinous' word *mōmos* at *Odyssey* 2.86 (as I discuss in detail in Chapter 4). From the vantage point of this interaction here (*Odyssey* 17.374–379 and 400), Antinous seems to resent Telemachus, first for begrudging the food the suitors eat, and secondly for reproaching them on this account (*Odyssey* 2.40–79) while extending generosity to a beggar. Telemachus' resounding response: οὔ τοι φθονέω, "I do not begrudge" (*Odyssey* 17.400) reiterates the deep-rooted belief that a benevolent king ought to extend hospitality to strangers and guests. By contrast, the suitors abuse both guests and hosts:

μνηστῆρες δ᾽ ἄρα πάντες ἐς ἀλλήλους ὁρόωντες
Τηλέμαχον ἐρέθιζον, ἐπὶ ξείνοις γελόωντες·
ὧδε δέ τις εἴπεσκε νέων ὑπερηνορεόντων·
"Τηλέμαχ᾽, οὔ τις σεῖο κακοξεινώτερος ἄλλος·
οἷον μέν τινα τοῦτον ἔχεις ἐπίμαστον ἀλήτην,
σίτου καὶ οἴνου κεχρημένον, οὐδέ τι ἔργων
ἔμπαιον οὐδὲ βίης, ἀλλ᾽ αὔτως ἄχθος ἀρούρης.
ἄλλος δ᾽ αὖτέ τις οὗτος ἀνέστη μαντεύεσθαι.
ἀλλ᾽ εἴ μοί τι πίθοιο, τό κεν πολὺ κέρδιον εἴη·
τοὺς ξείνους ἐν νηῒ πολυκληῗδι βαλόντες
ἐς Σικελοὺς πέμψωμεν, ὅθεν κέ τοι ἄξιον ἄλφοι."

They provoked Telemachus, laughing at his guests,
Thus someone[30] from among the overbearing youth kept upbraiding
    him:
"Telemachus, there is no one unluckier than you with guests.
You got this type here, a dirty wanderer,
yearning for food and wine, not skilled in any work
of peace or war, but rather he is a burden on the land.
Then this other one stands up and begins to prophesize!
But if you listen to me, it will be much to your advantage:
Let us throw these guests on a benched ship,
and send them to Sicily, which may be more profitable."

Odyssey 20.373-383

Antinous, along with all the suitors, deliberately provokes Telemachus (ἐρέθιζον, 374), inclined as he is to be quarrelsome.[31] Yet, his attacks against Telemachus' guests are specifically based on their low status (beggars and seers). Antinous' aristocratic bias draws a sharp distinction between the consuming suitors (his own band of chieftains) and the consuming beggars and seers, "devouring" commoners. By calling Telemachus a *kakoxeinos*, Antinous brings into question Telemachus' ability to be a discerning ruler, one who can properly distinguish between noble guests (the suitors), and ignoble ones (beggars). Thus, Antinous paints Telemachus as unfit for kingship on this point also. In other words, he censures Telemachus with disqualifying characteristics.

[30] As David Elmer pointed out to me in written correspondence, "These sentiments are attributed to the suitors in general, not specifically to Antinous. Or rather, it is an anonymous 'tis' [20.375] who speaks these words. But that anonymous 'somebody' seems to speak for the suitors as a whole."

[31] Just as Thersites is willing to fight (*erizemenai*) with kings (*Iliad* 2.247).

2.3 Telemachus *Nēpios,* or "Sometimes I Feel like a Fatherless Child"

Antinous often picks on Telemachus as though he were a child. His purpose is to strip Telemachus of his position and render him an ineffectual ruler.[32] While at times Telemachus does not respond to Antinous' tirades (*Odyssey* 20.385), at other times he seems to miss the point of the mockery:

> Ἀντίνο', εἴ πέρ μοι καὶ ἀγάσσεαι ὅττι κεν εἴπω,
> καί κεν τοῦτ' ἐθέλοιμι Διός γε διδόντος ἀρέσθαι.
> ἦ φὴς τοῦτο κάκιστον ἐν ἀνθρώποισι τετύχθαι;
> οὐ μὲν γάρ τι κακὸν βασιλευέμεν· αἶψά τέ οἱ δῶ
> ἀφνειὸν πέλεται καὶ τιμηέστερος αὐτός.

> Antinous, perhaps you might blame me for what I will say,
> I would gladly wish to receive this [kingship] if god would grant.
> Do you mean that this is the worst thing that could have been
> bestowed on mortals?
> For, it is not a bad thing to rule as a king. Immediately his household
> becomes wealthy and he himself very honorable.

> *Odyssey* 1.389–393

It is interesting to think that Telemachus' earnestness goes against the family grain, issuing as he does from a lineage of variously clever people—Odysseus *polumētis* "of many counsels" (*Odyssey* 21.274)[33] and his grandfather Autolycus, who exceled in thievery (*kleptosunēi*) and oaths (*horkōi* [*Odyssey* 19.396]). This difference in Telemachus' character corroborates the notion that he is disconnected from his family, as Edmunds argues in her analysis of the word *nēpios* in Homer.[34] I also associate *nēpios* and *ateleis* in that Telemachus is disconnected as long as he remains unaccomplished or unfulfilled (*atelēs*), that is, unfinished in ways that are considered essential for a ruler, in his case the future ruler. For example, Telemachus fails to speak in the assembly for a long time, lacking in authority, sometimes takes part in the suitors' feasts as though he were a

---

[32] Given the importance of being able to speak well in the context of the epic, not having the ability to make a proper *muthos*, or to hold an *epos* is tantamount to being blemished, that is, able to be satirized.

[33] See Haslam 1994:112 on the *Homer Lexicon* of Apollonius Sophista II for the two entries for *polumētis*: "πολύ[μητις: πολυγνώμων (much-knowing), πολύβουλος (much-planning), and πολύμητης: πολύβουλος, πολλὰ βουλεύσασθαι δύναμενος (able to plan/devise many things)."

[34] Edmunds 1990.

hetairos,[35] instead of the heir to the kingship, and finally he is almost out of time in searching for his father. Therefore, despite the suitors' ultimate failure in disqualifying Telemachus as Odysseus' successor, they do blemish him to a significant degree by highlighting his reluctance to act and speak. He is shown to be an heir to Ithaca who is, however, not quite fit for the position.

Telemachus is called *nēpios* various times in the *Odyssey*.[36] The word denotes "young child." Telemachus is childish, which is the quality that Antinous mocks by way of picking on his verbal inadequacy. In this respect, the sense of *nēpios* can be related to "not speaking" (*nē-epos*),[37] like the Latin word *infans* (infant), though there is no ancient authority for the attestation of this particular meaning.[38] The idea is just as well conveyed by the word *pais*, a "child" not necessarily "without speech" but without proper or mature speech. Moreover, the sense of *nēpios* as "inept," following Susan Edmunds, underscores Antinous' facetiousness when he says that Telemachus has been taught by the gods to "speak boldly" and that he might have grasped the gods' teaching only in style (... ἦ μάλα δή σε διδάσκουσιν θεοὶ αὐτοὶ / ὑψαγόρην τ' ἔμεναι καὶ θαρσαλέως ἀγορεύειν, *Odyssey* 1.384–385) but not in substance.[39] Therefore, the word *nēpios* in its application to Telemachus is relevant for my discussion of blame and satire. I start by looking at Telemachus' own perspective of his situation in the opening books.

When Athena asks Telemachus whether he is indeed Odysseus' son (*Odyssey* 1.206–207), he answers thus:

τοιγὰρ ἐγώ τοι, ξεῖνε, μάλ' ἀτρεκέως ἀγορεύσω.
μήτηρ μέν τ' ἐμέ φησι τοῦ ἔμμεναι, αὐτὰρ ἐγώ γε
οὐκ οἶδ'· οὐ γάρ πώ τις ἑὸν γόνον αὐτὸς ἀνέγνω.
ὡς δὴ ἐγώ γ' ὄφελον μάκαρός νύ τευ ἔμμεναι υἱὸς
ἀνέρος, ὃν κτεάτεσσιν ἑοῖς ἔπι γῆρας ἔτετμε.
νῦν δ' ὃς ἀποτμότατος γένετο θνητῶν ἀνθρώπων,
τοῦ μ' ἔκ φασι γενέσθαι, ἐπεὶ σύ με τοῦτ' ἐρεείνεις.

---

[35] See Hipponax fr. 115 W for the *ekhthros* who was once a *hetairos*.

[36] The suitors are also called *nēpioi*, but the meaning as applied to them is a general designation of foolishness, universally applied to human beings. In other words, no one is without fault, and thus everyone is foolish and vulnerable, a possible definition of mortality itself.

[37] This sense of *nēpios* as "not speaking" (*nē-epos*) is in fact given in the Greek-English Lexicon (1889, 1992. 7th ed). This analysis is not given in full in LSJ (1946:161).

[38] Chantraine (1968) sees no connection between *nēpios* and *nē-epos*: "Le sens 'qui ne sait parler' ne s'appuie sur aucune tradition ancienne (cf. *pourtant* νηπύτιον· νήπιον, ἄφωνον. . . et bien entendu aucun rapport ne doit être établi avec (ϝ)έπος)."

[39] *Tharsaleōs* here, as elsewhere in Homer, is ambivalent. *Thers/thars*, "bold" in both negative and positive senses. See 59-60n3.

Thus, I say to you, guest, truthfully indeed,
my mother, well, she says that I come from him, yet I actually
do not know:[40] for one himself does in no way know his own
     parentage.
I wish I were the blessed son
of a man whom old age cut down along with his possessions.
Now, though, he was born the most unfortunate of mortal men,
from him, they say that I was born, since you ask me this.

Odyssey 1.214–220

Athena's question is meant to recover Telemachus' identity as the hero's son,
but his answer reveals a measure of psychological struggle with his history, that
is, the absence of his father: "my mother, well, she says that I come from him,
yet I actually do not know" (*Odyssey* 1.215–216).[41] In these verses, Odysseus, the
missing limb that aches (so to speak), is effectively not named.[42] Telemachus has
been greatly hurt by his experience, and his development has been arrested, as
Athena points out later in the narrative:

φράζεσθαι δὴ ἔπειτα κατὰ φρένα καὶ κατὰ θυμὸν,
ὅππως κε μνηστῆρας ἐνὶ μεγάροισι τεοῖσι
κτείνῃς ἠὲ δόλῳ ἢ ἀμφαδόν· οὐδέ τί σε χρὴ
νηπιάας ὀχέειν, ἐπεὶ οὐκέτι τηλίκος ἐσσί.

Consider then in your mind and in your heart
how you might kill the suitors in your halls,
whether by a trick or openly; you must no longer
play childishly since you are not anymore of that age.

Odyssey 1.294–297

---

40 Compare the character Margites, cast as a simpleton who does not know whether it was his
    mother or father who had given birth to him (*Suda* 187); see Chapter 1, Section 2.

41 The expressions "I don't know" and "if I come from him" are also idiomatic, meant to convey
    how long it has been since Odysseus left. It does not really mean he does not know where he
    came from (compare in English "Hello, stranger" used to convey the same idea). However,
    Telemachus is "disconnected" in the sense Edmunds presents (1990: 45-46), as a result of his
    father's absence, thus the idiom carries wider significance.

42 Telemachus pictures Odysseus' absence, indeed, disappearance, as terrible fate: ἀνέρος, οὗ δή
    που λεύκ' ὀστέα πύθεται ὄμβρῳ / κεῖμεν' ἐπ' ἠπείρου, ἢ εἰν ἁλὶ κῦμα κυλίνδει, "of a man whose
    white bones rot somewhere in the rain / lying on the mainland, or the waves of the sea roll
    them" (*Odyssey* 1.161–162).

In Athena's role as a foster parent[43] to Telemachus, she challenges him to reclaim his real father: Telemachus must reclaim Odysseus, whether the hero is dead or alive (*Odyssey* 1.289–292). Athena helps Telemachus relate to his absent father by establishing a connection based on their physical resemblance: αἰνῶς μὲν κεφαλήν τε καὶ ὄμματα καλὰ ἔοικας / κείνῳ, ἐπεὶ θαμὰ τοῖον ἐμισγόμεθ' ἀλλήλοισι, "your head and beautiful eyes look amazingly like that man's, / for at that time, we often kept company with each other" (*Odyssey* 1.208–209).

Earlier in book 1 Athena makes her plans concerning Telemachus explicit to Zeus:

αὐτὰρ ἐγὼν Ἰθάκην ἐσελεύσομαι, ὄφρα οἱ υἱὸν
μᾶλλον ἐποτρύνω, καί οἱ μένος ἐν φρεσὶ θείω
εἰς ἀγορὴν καλέσαντα κάρη κομόωντας Ἀχαιοὺς
πᾶσι μνηστήρεσσιν ἀπειπέμεν

So now I will myself go to Ithaca, to encourage his son,
and put some daring [44] in his mind to summon into the assembly
the long-haired Achaeans and to speak out to all the suitors.

Odyssey 1.88–91

The objective of Athena's *paideia* is to teach Telemachus how to reconnect to his manhood, and she uses a combination of blame and admonition to nudge him into action. She compares Orestes' situation to Telemachus' and how the former achieved his *kleos* ("heroic glory" and "fame") by avenging his father's murderer, Aegisthus. Orestes, of course provides the perfect foil for Athena's admonition (*ainos*):

ἢ οὐκ ἀΐεις οἷον κλέος ἔλλαβε δῖος Ὀρέστης
πάντας ἐπ' ἀνθρώπους, ἐπεὶ ἔκτανε πατροφονῆα,
Αἴγισθον δολόμητιν, ὅ οἱ πατέρα κλυτὸν ἔκτα;
καὶ σύ, φίλος, μάλα γάρ σ' ὁρόω καλόν τε μέγαν τε,
ἄλκιμος ἔσσ', ἵνα τίς σε καὶ ὀψιγόνων ἐῢ εἴπῃ.

Or have you not heard of such glory that great Orestes received
among all men when he killed that patricide

---

[43] Although Telemachus was not subjected to exposure and fosterage abroad, his relationship to Athena establishes a kinship between goddess and hero. On divine fosterage, see the Etruscan bronze mirror of the late fourth century BCE (Museo Archeologico Nazionale, Tarquinia) depicting Hera nursing an adult Heracles, suggesting the hero's apotheosis into Olympus. Compare Edmunds 1990. For further questions on fosterage and kinship, see also Bremmer 1976; Parkes 2004.

[44] Compare 60n3 and 60n4 on *menos* as Latin *impetus* (daring).

Aegisthus, the deceitful, who had killed his glorious father?
And you also, friend, I see that you are you quite handsome and tall,[45]
be strong, so that someone in the future may also speak well of you.

Odyssey 1.298–302

Telemachus' journey can be interpreted more as a departure from child-hood than an achievement of manhood, and is articulated through the many ways he is referred to: son (*huios, Odyssey* 1.88), a child (*pais, Odyssey* 1.207), and an innocent baby (*nēpios, Odyssey* 4.818).[46] Telemachus' maturity and entry into adulthood will be completed when he is able to have both the courage (*menos*) and wisdom to match the epithet Athena used when addressing him (*pepnu-menos,* "wise").[47] In other words, Telemachus must be prepared to avenge his father's house against the outrageous takeover by the arrogant suitors. Like Orestes, he must be prepared to kill. He must also acquaint himself with the other veteran heroes from Troy, comrades of his father. These men—Nestor and Menelaus—act as foster fathers to him. They validate his identity, help him with resources (horses), and offer him a companion (Peisistratus). With them Telemachus will learn how to present himself properly and confidently:

τὴν δ᾽ αὖ Τηλέμαχος πεπνυμένος ἀντίον ηὔδα·
"Μέντορ, πῶς τ᾽ ἄρ᾽ ἴω, πῶς τ᾽ ἄρ προσπτύξομαι αὐτόν;
οὐδέ τί πω μύθοισι πεπείρημαι πυκινοῖσιν·
αἰδὼς δ᾽ αὖ νέον ἄνδρα γεραίτερον ἐξερέεσθαι."

So, to her again wise Telemachus answered:
Mentor, how then will I go? How will I search for him?
I am not at all experienced in fluent speech,
Moreover, it is shameful for a young man to speak out of turn to
    an elder.

Odyssey 3.21–24

---

[45] We will recall that Odysseus' handsomeness and tall stature are associated with his royal appear-ance (*Iliad* 3.191–224). Athena is using prospective and enthusiastic praise in order to encourage deeds worthy of a king. See Dumézil's 1943:43–44 observation on Indic epic myth where the thematic stress is on "la louange qualifiante," based not on past deeds, but on future ones. In other words, it raises expectations.

[46] See Clarke 1963.

[47] In the context of praise and blame, *pepnumenos,* though clearly an honorific title, can also function as *louange qualifiante* to one who is still a *nēpios.* Nevertheless, I submit that, despite Telemachus' voyage in search of his father and towards manhood, he never quite becomes the warrior-king fit to succeed Odysseus. Even after battling against the suitors, he still remains a child in everyone's eyes—for Odysseus, Penelope, and Eurycleia (*Odyssey* 20.134–137, 23.113–114).

Penelope also calls Telemachus *nēpios* because he does not yet know pain and sorrow or the gathering of adult men (*Odyssey* 4.818),[48] where adult men know how to hold an *epos*. However, it is now becoming unseemly for him not to act his age, as Athena points out. In other words, he must have his share of blame, whether constructively (by Athena) or destructively (by the suitors).[49] Therefore, at this point in the *Odyssey*, Telemachus deserves to be blamed as his condition of *nēpios* can no longer be acceptable, even if his situation is undoubtedly difficult. Eventually, however, he does come to stake his position both as an adult and as the royal heir. Accordingly, he declares that he is no longer a *nēpios*: ... ἤδη γὰρ νοέω καὶ οἶδα ἕκαστα, / ἐσθλά τε καὶ τὰ χέρεια· πάρος δ᾽ ἔτι νήπιος ἦα, "For now, I am aware, and I know each thing, / both good and bad, for I am no longer *nēpios* as before" (*Odyssey* 20.309–310). These verses not only reflect Telemachus' yearning for manhood, but more importantly, they express an ideology based on praise and blame, that is, a worldview that links nobility and knowledge. This conjunction of nobility and knowledge leads to praiseworthiness, the very quality highlighted in Hesiod as "kings who know" (*basileusin phroneousi*, *Works and Days* 202).[50] In other words, Telemachus sees himself becoming a king, not just as his birthright, but because he now has understanding. Telemachus is an interim king beset by more than one hundred satirists constantly demanding that which he cannot and should not give—his mother, Penelope, and the palace. The Irish tale "Guaire's Greedy Guests" offers an apt comparandum here, particularly in the equally outlandish number of guests (the company of poets) Guaire needs to keep happy. In both cases, their demands are unreasonable, their numbers intractable, and their language abusive. In the end they both pay for their illegitimate requests and wrongful words.[51]

---

[48] Penelope highlights the assembly as the adult male space where one would need to know how to speak well. Penelope is anxious about how her son might fare among the gathering of men because he is innocent (*nēpios*), thus by contrast, the assembly *agoreuōn* can be understood not only as the gathering where men speak, but also where they say corrupt, or threatening words.

[49] Consider again the meaning of the Greek word *teleios*—"complete," "fulfilled," "perfected"—and the notion of "Telemachus as *ateles*."

[50] Compare Bacchylides 3.85: φρονέοντι συνετὰ γαρύω, "I speak wisdom to the wise."

[51] Joynt 1941.

3

The Suit

3.1 Wooing and Contesting: The Institution of Courtship

The connection I have been establishing between Penelope's suitors and abusive language is this: the suitors in the *Odyssey* represent reproach and criticism, language that draws on the thematic and stylistic features of blame poetry. The suitors' language of criticism serves a political function: their struggle for the kingship of Ithaca. As I have indicated earlier, wooing (*mnēstus*) itself is often a catalyst for conflict, and in the *Odyssey* the courtship is presented in negative terms right from the start. Zeus recalls the famous suitor Aegisthus as an illustration of man's foolishness in their predisposition to blame the gods for their own recklessness and misfortunes (*Odyssey* 1.32–34). Aegisthus' tragic foolishness was to woo Clytemnestra, despite Hermes' warning against it (*Odyssey* 1.35–39). The reference to Aegisthus points to an even earlier myth concerning the curse against the house of Atreus, which will extend to the murder of Agamemnon.[1] The trajectory from the ill-fated wooing of Helen[2] to the war to rescue her begins with the Atreides' affairs in the distant past, and culminates with the heroes' "returns" (*nostoi*). Furthermore, Zeus' memory of Aegisthus and Clytemnestra offers a direct contrast between the fateful return of Agamemnon, and the survival of Odysseus about to be unfolded in the epic narrative. Finally, Zeus' interpretation of Aegisthus refocuses our attention toward the suitors' grievous wooing (*mnēstuos argaleēs*, *Odyssey* 2.199).[3] Zeus begins by addressing all

---

[1] Aeschylus *Agamemnon* 1590–1611.

[2] Paris, qua suitor, is the more terrible for having broken the sacred bonds of hospitality while a guest at Menelaus' house.

[3] Zeus' disapproving attitude towards wrongful wooing was also expressed in response to the feud between Atreus (Agamemnon's father) and his brother Thyestes. Atreus' wife, Aerope, had committed adultery with Thyestes and wished to transfer the kingship to him, but Zeus did not approve (Euripides *Electra* 699–746; Apollodorus *Epitome* 2.10–12).

the other gods with a speech (*muthos*) concerning the foolishness of Aegisthus as a suitor and of mortals generally:

τοῖσι δὲ μύθων ἦρχε πατὴρ ἀνδρῶν τε θεῶν τε·
μνήσατο γὰρ κατὰ θυμὸν ἀμύμονος Αἰγίσθοιο,
τόν ῥ' Ἀγαμεμνονίδης τηλεκλυτὸς ἔκταν' Ὀρέστης·
τοῦ ὅ γ' ἐπιμνησθεὶς ἔπε' ἀθανάτοισι μετηύδα·
"ὢ πόποι, οἷον δή νυ θεοὺς βροτοὶ αἰτιόωνται.
ἐξ ἡμέων γάρ φασι κάκ' ἔμμεναι. οἱ δὲ καὶ αὐτοὶ
σφῇσιν ἀτασθαλίῃσιν ὑπὲρ μόρον ἄλγε' ἔχουσιν,
ὡς καὶ νῦν Αἴγισθος ὑπὲρ μόρον Ἀτρεΐδαο
γῆμ' <u>ἄλοχον μνηστήν</u>, τὸν δ' ἔκτανε νοστήσαντα,
εἰδὼς αἰπὺν ὄλεθρον. πεὶ πρό οἱ εἴπομεν ἡμεῖς,
Ἑρμείαν πέμψαντες, εὔσκοπον ἀργειφόντην,
μήτ' αὐτὸν κτείνειν μήτε μνάασθαι ἄκοιτιν·
ἐκ γὰρ Ὀρέσταο τίσις ἔσσεται Ἀτρεΐδαο,
ὁππότ' ἂν ἡβήσῃ καὶ ἧς ἱμείρεται αἴης.
ὣς ἔφαθ' Ἑρμείας, ἀλλ' οὐ φρένας Αἰγίσθοιο
πεῖθ' ἀγαθὰ φρονέων· νῦν δ' ἀθρόα πάντ' ἀπέτισεν."

To them the father of gods and men started out with a *muthos*,
as he was reminded in his spirit of noble Aegisthus,
whom far-famed Agamemnon's son, Orestes, had slain.
As he thought about him, he spoke among the immortals, and said:
"Alas, how ready mortals are to blame the gods!
It is from us, they say, that evil things come, but it is they,
through their own blind folly, who have sorrows beyond measure,
even now[4] Aegisthus, beyond what was ordained,
married the <u>wooed-and-won</u>[5] <u>wife</u> of the son of Atreus and slew him
        on his return,
though he knew of the sheer destruction, since we told him before,
when we sent Hermes, the keen-sighted Argeiphontes,
to warn him neither to slay the man nor woo his wife:
from Orestes vengeance would come for the son of Atreus
once he [Orestes] achieved manhood and longed for his own land.

---

[4] The adverbial expression ὡς καὶ νῦν ("as even now") sets the time frame for Zeus' thoughts, if not his speech, to be simultaneous with Aegisthus' folly, as it moved from illicit marriage to the killing of Agamemnon. This Olympian point of view represents Zeus' mind pondering over the various heroes' fates, and as the god speaks, his will unfolds.

[5] I have chosen to translate *mnēstēn* as "wooed-and-won" so that it reflects the inherent presence of *agōn* in wooing. The discussion that follows will elucidate this point.

So, Hermes spoke, but the mind of Aegisthus
he did not persuade to consider good things: and now he has paid
   the full price."[6]

Odyssey 1.28–41

In Zeus' speech the word αἰτιάομαι (line 32) is the verb used in reference to the sort of blame that points to the original cause of a conflict.[7] Thus, αἰτιάομαι and *aitia* come closer to the juridical sense that we find in the Latin verb *accusare*. Although, not on the same register as the diction used in the conventional language of blame poetry, such as reproach (*oneidizō*) or blame/begrudging *mōmaomai*, the term is not value neutral in this context. Indeed, Zeus highlights its negative value, because it points to the cause of the destruction (*aipun olethron*, line 37) caused by Aegisthus' inability to turn his mind to good counsel (*agatha phroneōn*, line 41). Zeus makes it clear that Aegisthus had been forewarned by Hermes not to kill Agamemnon and woo (*mnaasthai*, line 37) Clytemnestra. His disobedience and disregard of the god's injunctions were the *aitia* of his (and others') suffering. Orestes' relationship to Aegisthus is analogous to Telemachus' relationship to the suitors. Orestes' killing of Aegisthus is an expected consequence of that suitor's arrogance. Thus, Zeus' speech foreshadows what will happen to Penelope's suitors and sets up the very institution of wooing as potentially, if not inherently, violent and dangerous, a demonstration of the effects of *hubris* committed against the gods' will. Indeed, the suitors are often referred to as *hubristai* (*Odyssey* 6.120, 9.175, 13.201, 24.282).

On the level of language, there is a critical convergence between two key words: the first, *mnaasthai* ("to woo"), from the second meaning of μνάομαι = μιμνήσκω (μιμνήσκομαι in middle and passive forms) "to be reminded, to remember"; the second, *mnaomai* ("to recall," "remind oneself," or "call to mind"), from μνάομαι, causal of μέμνημαι < μιμνήσκω. Both verbs—"to woo" and "to be reminded"—share the same *mn- root and are connected to each other semantically as well. Accordingly, in Zeus' s speech we find a fair number of verbs denoting such mental activities. Zeus "recalls," "thinks of" (*mnēsato*, line 29; *epimnēstheis*, line 31) and starts with a story (*muthōn ērkhe*, line 28) about a suitor, who "against divine orders" (*huper moron*, line 35), married a married woman, "wooed-and-won" (*mnēstēn*, line 36). The god had warned Aegisthus

---

[6]   Translation adapted from the Loeb Classical Library.

[7]   See Herodotus' discussion of *aitia* in connection with the Persian wars, with each side taking revenge against the latest outrage done by the other, i.e. the alternating kidnapping of women, now by the Greeks, now by the Persians, starting from Argive Io taken to Egypt, then Europa taken from Phoenicia to Crete, next Medea from Colchis, and finally Helen of Sparta to Troy (1.2.1–2).

not to "direct his thoughts" toward Clytemnestra nor "to woo" her, but Zeus did not persuade (*peith'*) his (Aegisthus') mind. Therefore, wooing can be understood as a special kind of thinking, directed toward winning in marriage (*gameō*) the contested (*mnēstēn*) woman at a high price. In a sense, wooing comes closer to plotting and strategizing, concepts that fit Penelope's suitors as they plot Telemachus' death (*Odyssey* 20.241–242) in order to remove him as an obstacle to their pursuit of bride and kingship.[8]

We can now express the connection between blame, satire, and wooing in this way: satire can be understood as a discourse aiming at injuring its victim, which sometimes involves the pursuit of a woman and the pursuit of power. The semantic range of *mnaasthai* in *Odyssey* 1.39 include mental strategies for eliminating the competition, and wooing.[9] From the suitors' point of view, thinking strategically in order to "woo and win" is necessary because women not only may have various suitors, but also resist marriage, as does the famous Atalanta, for instance:

> ... ποδώκης δῖ' Ἀταλάν[τη
> ... Χαρί]των ἀμαρύγματ' ἔχο[υσα
> πρὸς ἀνθρώπων ἀ]παναίνετο φῦλον ὁμιλ[εῖν
> ἀνδρῶν ἐλπομένη φεύγ]ειν γάμον ἀλφηστάων[.

> swift-footed godlike Atalanta
> of radiant glance .... from the Graces
> refused to come together with the race of mortal men
> hoping to escape marriage with enterprising ambitious men.

> Hesiod *Catalogue of Women* 73.2–5 M-W[10]

---

[8] For a relevant comparandum, see "The Wooing of Luaine and Death of Athirne" in Stokes 1868, 1903. Athirne performs an unjust satire which causes unsightly blotches on the woman he is pursuing. For this unjust satire Athirne meets his death.

[9] Another term for wooing perhaps closer to the notion of strategizing is *peiraō*, "attempt," "try," "test." In Hesiod's *Catalogue of Women*, a fragment describes Sisyphus' strategy to secure a woman for his son: τῆς μὲν Σίσυφο]ς Αἰολίδης πειρήσατο, βουλέων / βοῦς ἐλάσα[ς ἀλλ' οὔ τι Διὸ]ς νόον αἰγιόχοιο ἔγνω) "Sisyphus, son of Aelous tested her [=daughter of Pandion] plans by driving the oxen, but in no way did he know the mind of the aegis-bearing Zeus" [that no descendant should come to Sisyphus] (*Catalogue of Women* 43a.75–77 M-W). At *Odyssey* 19.215, Penelope tells Odysseus that she will *test* him (*peirēsesthai*), and here too the word is connected to wooing. Testing Odysseus is a necessary step in the direction of confirming the hero as the winning suitor, the one with the power to eliminate the competition.

[10] Merkelbach and West 1990.

To escape marriage is of course what Penelope attempts to do with her delay tactics, until she fears she can no longer "escape marriage" (ἐκφυγέειν [*Odyssey* 19.157]).

The wooing of Helen in Hesiod's *Catalogue of Women* (frr. 196–204 M-W) offers an especially good illustration of calculated thinking on the part of her suitors. While the verb *emnato* (he wooed) is used of all of Helen's suitors (e.g. Philoctetes, the twin sons of Amphiaraus, and Idomeneus), not all suitors wooed the same way, and all seemed to have a strategy.[11] For example, we are told that the chief Idomeneus from Crete did not send any intermediary but came himself (ἀλλ' αὐτὸς, fr. 204.59 M-W) in his black ship. By contrast, some suitors did send envoys, notably Agamemnon who came on behalf of his brother Menelaus, the ultimate winning suitor.

We hear about a similar conflict in Euripides' play *Iphigenia at Aulis* concerning Clytemnestra, Agamemnon's "wooed and won" (ἄλοχον μνηστήν) wife (*Odyssey* 1.36). In the play, Clytemnestra is reproaching (ὀνειδίσω) Agamemnon for marrying and taking her "by force" and "against her will" (ἔγημας ἄκουσάν με κἄλαβες βίᾳ) from her first husband Tantalus (*Iphigenia at Aulis* 1148–1150).[12] The connection between suitors (*mnēstēres*) and competitive struggle (*agōn*) is traditional and well attested. We find various instances of the pairing or juxtaposition of *mnēstēres* and *agōn*, as in the example in Pindar below:[13]

οἷοι Λιβύσσας ἀμφὶ γυναικὸς ἔβαν
Ἴρασα πρὸς πόλιν, Ἀνταίου μετὰ καλλίκομον
μναστῆρες ἀγακλέα κούραν·
τὰν μάλα πολλοὶ ἀριστῆες ἀνδρῶν αἴτεον
σύγγονοι, πολλοὶ δὲ καὶ ξείνων. ἐπεὶ θαητὸν εἶδος
ἔπλετο· χρυσοστεφάνου δέ οἱ Ἥβας
καρπὸν ἀνθήσαντ' ἀποδρέψαι
ἔθελον. πατὴρ δὲ θυγατρὶ φυτεύων
κλεινότερον γάμον, ἄκουσεν Δαναόν ποτ' ἐν Ἄργει
οἷον εὗρεν τεσσαράκοντα καὶ ὀκτὼ παρθένοισι πρὶν μέσον
            ἆμαρ ἑλεῖν,

---

[11] Odysseus' strategy was to bring no gifts, possibly because he knew the odds were inevitably in favor of Menelaus (*Catalogue* 198.4–6 M-W).

[12] The suggestion is that Agamemnon raped Clytemnestra; thereby we find another direct connection between wooing and violence.

[13] Other examples include variants on the theme of contest, with diction that likewise signifies conflict and struggle: μνηστεύειν ... ἐρίσωσιν ("they woo and quarrel," *Odyssey* 18.277). Compare πικροῦ... μνηστῆρος ("of a bitter suitor," Aeschylus *Prometheus Bound* 739–740); εὐκλεᾶ λαοσσόων μναστῆρ' ἀγώνων ("a noble suitor of the contest," Pindar *Pythian* 12.24).

ὠκύτατον γάμον. ἔστασεν γὰρ ἅπαντα χορὸν
ἐν τέρμασιν αὐτίκ' ἀγῶνος·
σὺν δ' ἀέθλοις ἐκέλευσεν διακρῖναι ποδῶν,
ἅντινα σχήσοι τις ἡρώων, ὅσοι γαμβροί σφιν ἦλθον.
οὕτω δ' ἐδίδου Λίβυς ἁρμόζων κόρᾳ
νυμφίον ἄνδρα· ποτὶ γραμμᾷ μὲν αὐτὰν στᾶσε κοσμήσαις τέλος ἔμμεν
    ἄκρον,
εἶπε δ' ἐν μέσσοις ἀπάγεσθαι, ὃς ἂν πρῶτος θορὼν
ἀμφί οἱ ψαύσειε πέπλοις.

For the sake of the Libyan woman they went
to the city of Irasa as suitors, in pursuit of the famous daughter of
    Antaeus, the one with beautiful hair.
Indeed, a number of the best men were pursuing her,
neighbors and foreigners alike because her shinning beauty
was perfect. The blossoming fruit of her Youth crowned with gold,
    this the men
wished to pluck. But her father, conceiving for his daughter a more
illustrious marriage, heard about Danaus, of how in Argos
he found marriage for his forty-eight daughters, before midday, the
    speediest affair.
He quickly lined up the whole band of women
at the turning post [of the competition].
With prizes he ordered them to decide with the foot race,
That each of the heroes would have a wife, as many as those who
    came to become his sons-in-law.
In this way, the Libyan [Antaeus] set it up, joining a groom to each girl
Adorning her. He [Antaeus] stood her each one at the end post to be
    the final prize.
In their midst he said that the winner would be the first one to leap
and touch her dress.

Pindar Pythian 9.105–120

In this passage, we find *mnastēres* (in Pindar's Doric dialect, in contrast to *mnēsteres* in Homer) and *agōn* semantically and ritualistically connected, as the competition for a bride becomes an athletic event, complete with the "goalpost," *gramma* (the woman herself), reminiscent of the turning post, *sēma* (*Iliad* 23.326) in the chariot race (*Iliad* 23.306–348). Other words also signify suitors and contest, such as the "best men" (*aristēes*, line 107), "famous marriage" (*kleinoteron gamon*, line 112), "at the turning post" (*en termasin*, line 114), "the whole band" (*hapanta khoron,* line 114), "decide," "judge" (*diakrinai,* line 115), "of the footraces" (*podōn,* line 115), "sons-in-law" (*gambroi,* line 116), "with prizes" (*aethlois,* line 115), and "the first one" (*prōtos,* line 119). Pindar praises the victor's ancestors, who traveled to Irasa as the *mnastēres* of Antaeus' beautiful daughters. Antaeus modeled the race contest after another story about suitors and contest, that of Danaus, used as a point of comparison (οἶον εὗρεν [113]... οὕτω [117]).

In *Pythian* 12, we see "contest" paired with "suitor," and the relationship establishes the flute (standing for song) as the "suitor," and the "public contest" as the object of desire:

εὗρεν θεός· ἀλλά νιν εὑροῖσ' ἀνδράσι θνατοῖς ἔχειν,
ὠνύμασεν κεφαλᾶν πολλᾶν νόμον,
εὐκλεᾶ <u>λαοσσόων μναστῆρ' ἀγώνων</u>,

The goddess [Athena] discovered it [the flute],
but she discovered it for mortal men to have
named it the many-headed[14] melody,
the glorious <u>wooer of public contests</u>.

Pindar Pythian 12.22–24

Likewise, an explicit example of the theme of the struggling suitor, articulated with diction that includes the pairing of *mnēstēres* and *agōn,* comes from Sophocles' *Trachiniae.* We see how Deianeira feared her suitor, the river god Achelous, and how Heracles battled him. Although Heracles was not himself the intended suitor (think of Odysseus and Nausicaa), Deianeira was given to him as a prize bride. Deianeira does not want to marry her suitor, Achelous, because he is undesirable both in his various forms appearing now as a bull, a dragon, now as an ox-face creature, and because of his persistence: "he was always asking my father" (Sophocles *Trachiniae* 8). And thus, the stage is set for struggle:

ἥτις πατρὸς μὲν ἐν δόμοισιν Οἰνέως
ναίουσ' ἔτ' ἐν Πλευρῶνι νυμφείων ὄτλον.
ἄλγιστον ἔσχον, εἴ τις Αἰτωλὶς γυνή.
<u>μνηστὴρ</u> γὰρ ἦν μοι ποταμός, Ἀχελῷον λέγω,
ὅς μ' ἐν τρισὶν μορφαῖσιν ἐξῄτει πατρός,

---

[14] The reference is to the gorgon whom Perseus killed. The poet is celebrating Midas of Acragas, the victor of the flute-playing contest. In this mythological interlude the poet recalls the invention of the flute by Pallas Athena inspired by the sound of the gorgon's shrills (Euryale in particular). As it is conventional for Pindar's victory odes to weave elaborate mythological references, the term interlude can be almost misleading. It is, at times, more appropriate as a designation to the part of poem that falls outside the myth.

φοιτῶν ἐναργὴς ταῦρος, ἄλλοτ' αἰόλος
δράκων ἑλικτός, ἄλλοτ' ἀνδρείῳ κύτει
βούπρωρος· ἐκ δὲ δασκίου γενειάδος
κρουνοὶ διερραίνοντο κρηναίου ποτοῦ
τοιόνδ' ἐγὼ <u>μνηστῆρα</u> προσδεδεγμένη
δύστηνος ἀεί. κατθανεῖν ἐπηυχόμην,
πρὶν τῆσδε κοίτης ἐμπελασθῆναί ποτε.
χρόνῳ δ' ἐν ὑστέρῳ μέν, ἀσμένη δέ μοι,
ὁ κλεινὸς ἦλθε Ζηνὸς Ἀλκμήνης τε παῖς·
ὃς εἰς <u>ἀγῶνα</u> τῷδε συμπεσὼν <u>μάχης</u>
ἐκλύεταί με. καὶ τρόπον μὲν ἂν <u>πόνων</u>
οὐκ ἂν διείποιμ'· οὐ γὰρ οἶδ'· ἀλλ' ὅστις ἦν
θακῶν ἀταρβὴς τῆς θέας, ὅδ' ἂν λέγοι·
ἐγὼ γὰρ ἤμην ἐκπεπληγμένη φόβῳ
μή μοι τὸ κάλλος ἄλγος ἐξεύροι ποτέ.
τέλος δ' ἔθηκε <u>Ζεὺς ἀγώνιος</u> καλῶς,

For while I still was dwelling in the house
of my father Oeneus at Pleuron, I had fear of marriage
most distressing fear, as never any woman of Aetolia had.
For my <u>suitor</u> was a river, Achelous, I mean,
who, taking on three shapes, was always asking my father for my
        hand in marriage—
coming now as a bull in visible form, now as a serpent,
slippery and coiled, now ox-faced with human trunk,
while from his thick-shaded beard
wellheads of fountain water sprayed.
In the expectation that such a <u>suitor</u> would get me,
I was always praying in my misery that I might die,
before I should ever approach that marriage bed.
But sometime later, to my joy,
the glorious child of Zeus and Alcmene [Heracles] came,
and he, joining in <u>struggle of battle</u> with him [the river god, Achelous],
set me free. And what kind of <u>struggle</u> it was
I could not describe, for I do not know. But if there was anyone
sitting nearby, unafraid of that sight, he could tell it;
for I sat stricken with terror, lest
my beauty might bring sorrow down upon me.
Finally <u>Zeus patron of contests</u> decided well.

Sophocles *Trachiniae* 6–26

The pairing of *agōn* (line 20) and *makhēs* (line 21) describes how Heracles, the glorious hero (*ho kleinos*, line 19) battles Achelous, Deianeira's suitor (*mnēstēra*, line 15). To be a suitor is to inevitably enter into contested struggle.

Another example of this paradigm is in the poem *Alexandra*, which details Cassandra's prophecies. There we see how marriage is a burden to young women, who on their part want to escape their marriage. The *Alexandra*—interestingly enough—mentions the physical attributes of potential suitors, and the word *mōmar* (poetic for *mōmos*) is used to disparage the unattractive men:

κοῦραι δὲ παρθένειον <u>ἐκφυγεῖν ζυγὸν</u>
ὅταν θέλωσι, νυμφίους ἀρνούμεναι
τοὺς Ἐκτορείοις ἠγλαϊσμένους κόμαις,
μορφῆς ἔχοντας <u>σίφλον</u> ἢ <u>μῶμαρ</u> γένους,
ἐμὸν περιπτύξουσιν ὠλέναις βρέτας,
ἄλκαρ μέγιστον κτώμεναι νυμφευμάτων,
Ἐρινύων ἐσθῆτα καὶ ῥέθους βαφὰς
πεπαμέναι θρόνοισι φαρμακτηρίοις.
κείναις ἐγὼ δηναιὸν ἄφθιτος θεὰ
ῥαβδηφόροις γυναιξὶν αὐδηθήσομαι.

And young girls, as to the yoke of girlhood,
whenever they wish to <u>escape marriage</u>, refusing bridegrooms
those with shinning hair like Hector's,
those who have physical <u>blemish</u> [*siphlos*], or <u>defect</u> of lineage [*mōmar*],
these girls will embrace my wooden image with their arms,
and will win the greatest defense against marriage:
the clothes of the Erinyes , and their faces
painted with magical herbs.
Then I will be called immortal goddess by them,
The women who carry the staff.

Lycophron Alexandra 1131–1141

In various other myths, suitors often meet with a dreadful fate at the hands of fathers managing the contest for their daughters. Hippodamia's father, Oenomaus, would slay all the suitors whom he could overtake in his chariot race, until Pelops managed to win her (Apollodorus *Epitome* 2.4).[15] Oenopion gouged Orion's eyes, when this man came to Chios to woo his daughter Merope

---

[15] See Pindar on this myth: ἐπεὶ τρεῖς τε καὶ δέκ' μναστῆρας ὀλέσαις / ἀναβάλλεται γάμον / θυγατρός, "having killed thirteen suitors, he [father Oenomaus] delays the wedding" (*Olympian* 1.79–81).

(Apollodorus *Library* 1.4.3), and Schoneus wishes that Hippomenes will always remember how difficult the contest was to win his daughter, Atalanta:[16]

> Hippomenes seeks (μνηστεύει) my coy-eyed daughter to wife; but let him now hear my wholesome speech. He shall not win her *without contest* (ἀεθλου ἄτερ), yet, if he be victorious and *escape death* (θάνατοντε φύγη), and if the deathless gods who dwell on Olympus grant him to win renown, verily he shall return to his dear native land, and I will give him my dear child and strong, swift-footed horses besides, which he shall lead home to be cherished possessions; and may he rejoice in heart possessing these, and *ever remember* with gladness the *painful contest* (ἀνιηρὸν ἄεθλον μεμνέωτ᾽ εὐφροσύνῃσι). . . for she, even fair and swift-footed, ran scorning the gifts of golden Aphrodite; but with him [Hippomenes] the race was *for his life* (περὶ ψυχῆς), either *to find his doom* (μόρον εὑρεῖν) or *to escape it* (φυγεῖν). Therefore, with thoughts of *guile* (δολοφρονέων) he said to her: "O daughter of Schoeneus, pitiless in heart, receive these glorious gifts of the goddess, golden Aphrodite"
>
> Hesiod *Catalogue of Women* 14. 10-29 = frr. 75.14-25;
> 76.1-10 M-W[17]

The verb form *memneōto* ("let him keep in mind") echoes *mnēsteuei* ("he woos"), and this connection represents the primary concerns and anxieties of a suitor. The fates of all suitors are variable, but death (*thanatos*) is always lurking. They may die either in the process of wooing (Pindar *Olympian* 1.75–81), or afterwards in the exacting of revenge (Orestes' killing of Aegisthus). Indeed, the death of Agamemnon can be linked to the killing of suitors as a theme as he won Clytemnestra (*klute-mnēst[r]ē*, "famously wooed" wife), a woman already won and married, just as Aegisthus did after him. The wooing of Clytemnestra, like many others, was an act of subduing, a contentious, violent, and wrongful act against which Zeus himself had forewarned.[18]

To be sure, wooing and seeking marriage encompass varying degrees of agonistic intensity and danger. In the *Odyssey*, this danger is vividly expressed by the adjectives *ōkumoroi* and *pikrogamoi* (respectively, "doomed" and "bitter

---

[16] In Apollodorus' version of the myth of Atalanta, her father is Isos, not Schoeneus (*Library* 3.9.2). But the story of the contest is the same, although Apollodorus does not report any speech by Isos.

[17] Merkelbach and West 1967. Translation by Hugh G. Evelyn-White is from the Loeb edition of *Hesiod: The Homeric Hymn and Homerica* (1970).

[18] In this connection, compare the various instances of women "subdued" by their suitors (*hupodmētheisa*, fr.25.18) in the *Catalogue of Women*, such as Deianeira (25.17–18 M-W), to name just one.

marriage," *Odyssey* 4.346; 17.137)[19] to refer to what will be the suitors' fate at the hand of Odysseus: τοῖος ἐὼν μνηστῆρσιν ὁμιλήσειεν Ὀδυσσεύς / πάντες κ' ὠκύμοροί τε γενοίατο πικρόγαμοί τε, "I wish my father such as he is would come together among the suitors / All of them would become damned and obtain bitter marriage" (*Odyssey* 1.265–266).

Sometimes, wooing is a straightforward competition, where the clear winner takes the bride, as with Alexidamus taking Antaeus' daughter (Pindar *Pythian* 9). At other times, it is risky and difficult, as with Pelops and Hippodamia (Apollodorus *Library* 2.4–6). Sometimes the taking of the bride is by force (Clytemnestra by Agamemnon), sometimes by deceit (Atalanta by Hippomenes). It may also include the maiming or killing of suitors (Oenopion and Oenomaus, respectively). Against such a grim mythopoetic background, the *Odyssey*'s *mnēstērophonia*[20] represents the Homeric expression of a tradition where suitors woo brides and win lands through struggle, at the risk of death. In the *Odyssey*, the locus classicus for the competitive struggle inherent in courtship is the famous stringing of the bow, but just as prominent are the pervasive insults, and abusive words exchanged between the suitors, Odysseus, and Telemachus. In the end, Odysseus competes for and wins Penelope for a second time.

Since the Homeric suitors are unheroic, their words are reproachful, abusive, and expressed with iambic sentiment, in contrast to the heroic boasts which often attend the *aristeia* of warriors.[21] In the lyric poetry of Pindar, with its embedded mythological stories, the suitors are typically presented as subjects or objects of speeches, while in the *Odyssey* they are often themselves the speakers of their own predicament. We hear them directly as they reproach and mock anyone who stands in the way of their conquest of both Penelope and Ithaca. Thus, the verbal adjective *mnēstēn,* designating "wedded" as the result of "wooing and winning," represents the conflation of the martial and erotic realms with the political and social realms of marriage (*gamos*). In Zeus' speech in book 1, we find the juxtaposition between *mnēstēn* and *gamein:* ὡς

---

[19] In effect, "bitter marriage" is often synonymous with marriage itself when the young woman sees it as an undesirable burden, as I have pointed out above.

[20] For the use of the term *mnēstērophonia*, see Strabo 1.2.2; Athenaeus 5.192d; for both *mnēstērophonia* and *mnēstēroktonia*, see Eustathius, *Commentaries* I 88 (Cullhed 2006:104). Odysseus then can be described as a *mnēstēroktonos*, as is Hippodamia's father, Oenomaus (Apollodorus *Epitome* 2.4). See Rosen 2003:122–123 for his discussion of Thersites' death at the hands of Achilles, depicted on a fourth-century BCE Apulian vase representing the quarrel between Achilles and Thersites, entitled the *Thersitoktonos* vase. On the description of the vase and its relation to a fourth-century tragedy BCE called *Achilles Thersitoktonos*, see Taplin 2014:154. On this painting (based on the tragedy posited to be by Chaeremon), the Erinys standing over Thersites' dead body is labeled *Poina*, "Vengeance" (Padel 1994).

[21] *Iliad* 16.619–625 (Meriones taunts Aeneas); *Iliad* 16. 830–842 (Hector boasts over the slain Patroclus).

καὶ νῦν Αἴγισθος ὑπὲρ μόρον Ἀτρεΐδαο / γῆμ' ἄλοχον μνηστήν, τὸν δ' ἔκτανε
νοστήσαντα, "just as now Aegisthus, beyond what is right, / married the *wooed-
and-won* wife of Atreus' son, and killed him upon his return." (*Odyssey* 1.35–36).

There is a curious example of the juxtaposition between wooing and
marriage in book 6 of the *Iliad*. While *mnēstēis alokhoisin* at 6.246 ("wooed and
won") is used of Priam's daughters-in-law, *aidoiēis alokhoisin* at 6.250 ("reverent
wives") describes Priam's own daughters. While the difference between *mnēstēis*
and *aidoiēis* may indicate poetic variation on the same theme, the contrast seems
to privilege the success of Priam's sons as suitors over his sons-in-law.

3.2 Wrongful Wooing

Zeus' *muthos* concerning the wrongful and violent wooing of Clytemnestra by
Aegisthus can be understood as a cautionary tale, an *ainos*. Athena interrupts
Zeus' ponderings about Agamemnon's return and reminds him of Odysseus' fate
and that of his son. She explains that the suitors are killing off Telemachus'
sheep and oxen (*Odyssey* 1.92), thereby establishing the core problem at
Penelope's palace: the devouring of Odysseus' wealth. The suitors in effect stage
an aggressive "sitting and waiting,"[22] during which time they take possession of
Odysseus' riches—the *unmoveable* and the *moveable* kinds, κειμήλιά τε πρόβασίν
τε (*Odyssey* 2.75), as Telemachus puts it.[23] Non-movables are those things that
cannot move by themselves, such as weapons, and the enslaved person who is
not free to move, while moveable are oxen and pigs (presumably more free to
move than slaves). Notwithstanding the division of wealth into these two cate-
gories, the emphasis on the consumption of oxen and pigs (the moveable riches)
over other goods turns *probata* into a designation for all wealth collectively.[24] In
poetic terms, the gluttonous suitors destroy everything along with oxen and
pigs (*minutheskon edontes*).

---

[22] As I mentioned earlier, this *sitting and waiting* is expedient from the point of view of the narrative, allowing time for Odysseus' return and the final competition among suitors (the stringing
of the bow). Waiting also heightens the level of transgression to the point of saturation, which
further justifies their impending violent death.

[23] Watkins 1995:9–10 cites this passage when he discusses the formula "goods and chattels": "This
formula is a merism, a two-part figure which makes reference to the totality of a single concept
... goods and chattels, non-moveable and moveable wealth together designate all wealth ... We
find a semantically identical formula in Homeric Greek ... the phrase κειμήλιά τε πρόβασίν τε
(*Odyssey* 2.75), where Telemachus complains of the suitors devouring his 'riches which lie and
riches which move,' the totality of his wealth." See Benveniste 1969:43–45.

[24] For unmovable goods (κειμήλια), Benveniste 1969:43 includes "precious metals, gold, leather,
iron."

The link Athena establishes between agonistic wooing (*mnaomai*) and destructive feasting (*dainumii*) find its poetic articulation among the suitors themselves at *Odyssey* 20.246: ἀλλὰ μνησώμεθα δαιτός, "but let us *turn our minds* to the feast." To put it another way, the phrase could be understood as a kind of epitome of the suitors' role: they woo and feast. The two passages below illustrate this:

1.) τοῖσι δὲ κήρυκες μὲν ὕδωρ ἐπὶ χεῖρας ἔχευαν,
   σῖτον δὲ δμῳαὶ παρενήνεον ἐν κανέοισιν,
   κοῦροι δὲ κρητῆρας ἐπεστέψαντο ποτοῖο.
   οἱ δ' ἐπ' ὀνείαθ' ἑτοῖμα προκείμενα χεῖρας ἴαλλον.
   αὐτὰρ ἐπεὶ πόσιος καὶ ἐδητύος ἐξ ἔρον ἔντο
   μνηστῆρες, τοῖσιν μὲν ἐνὶ φρεσὶν ἄλλα μεμήλει,
   μολπή τ' ὀρχηστύς τε· τὰ γὰρ τ' ἀναθήματα δαιτός.

And heralds poured water on their [the suitors'] hands,
while the maids set the food into baskets,
and boys filled cups with drink.
Next, they laid their hands to the meal lying before them,
and when their thirst and hunger were satisfied
the suitors turned their minds to other things,
to song and dance: for these things are the accompaniment of
   the feast.

Odyssey 1.146–152

2.) εὗρε δ' ἄρα μνηστῆρας ἀγήνορας. οἱ μὲν ἔπειτα
   πεσσοῖσι προπάροιθε θυράων θυμὸν ἔτερπον,
   ἥμενοι ἐν ῥινοῖσι βοῶν, οὓς ἔκτανον αὐτοί·
   κήρυκες δ' αὐτοῖσι καὶ ὀτρηροὶ θεράποντες
   οἱ μὲν ἄρ' οἶνον ἔμισγον ἐνὶ κρητῆρσι καὶ ὕδωρ.
   οἱ δ' αὖτε σπόγγοισι πολυτρήτοισι τραπέζας
   νίζον καὶ πρότιθεν, τοὶ δὲ κρέα πολλὰ δατεῦντο.

And she found the proud suitors. At that moment they were
delighting their spirit with games, sitting by the front doors
on the hides of oxen, which they themselves had slaughtered.
The heralds served them, and also attending cupbearers,
mixing wine and water in large cups.
And some were scrubbing tables with porous sponges,
arranging them, while others distributed plenty of meat.

Odyssey 1.106–112

Passages 1 and 2 would offer a vivid description of the suitors as revelers, but the contrast between "delighted" (*eterpon*) and "slaughtered" (*ektanon*) is sharp. In their reveling, their enemies suffer while their companions laugh:

τοῖσιν δ' Εὐρύμαχος, Πολύβου πάϊς, ἄρχ' ἀγορεύειν
κερτομέων Ὀδυσῆα· γέλω δ' ἐτάροισιν ἔτευχε.

To them, Eurymachus, son of Polybus, started to speak,
mocking Odysseus and bringing laughter to his companions.

Odyssey 18.349–350

The more outlandish they become in their mockery, the more Odysseus' revenge will seem justified, even if extreme. Athena makes the suitors especially vicious in the hope to infuse Odysseus with a more intense desire for retribution:

μνηστῆρας δ' οὐ πάμπαν ἀγήνορας εἴα Ἀθήνη
λώβης ἴσχεσθαι θυμαλγέος, ὄφρ' ἔτι μᾶλλον
δύη ἄχος κραδίην Λαερτιάδεω Ὀδυσῆος.

Not at all did Athena restrain the proud suitors
from carrying on soul-wrenching insult, so that even more
grief would sink deeper into the heart of Odysseus, son of Laertes.

Odyssey 18. 346–348

Penelope herself has the occasion to reproach Antinous for his plotting and outrageous lack of restraint: τοῦ νῦν οἶκον ἄτιμον ἔδεις, μνάᾳ δὲ γυναῖκα / παῖδά τ' ἀποκτείνεις, ἐμὲ δὲ μεγάλως ἀκαχίζεις, "Now you devour his [Odysseus'] dishonored house, and court his wife / and even plan to murder his son—you distress me greatly" (16.431–432).

In response to Telemachus' speech at the assembly in book 2, the suitors begin to act more boldly. Telemachus' call to a new order triggers a set of speeches by the suitors (*Odyssey* 2.85–145; 2.161–176; 2.178–207; 2.209–223; 2.229–256), which resemble verbal dueling in structure, and aim at neutralizing his position:[25]

    a. Antinous rebukes Telemachus (2.85–128)

    b. Telemachus responds (2.129–145)

    c. Halitherses defends Telemachus' cause (2.161–176)

    a¹. Eurymachus rebukes Halitherses (2.178–207)

---

[25] See Martin 1989:65–77 on verbal dueling and poetics of flyting. See also Pagliai 2009; Agovi 1985.

b¹. Telemachus responds (2.209–223)

c¹. Mentor defends Telemachus/reproaches the people (2.229–241)

a². Leocritus rebukes Mentor (2.242–256)

At the end of these exchanges, Antinous clasps Telemachus' hand in feigned friendship while the others laugh (*Odyssey* 2.301–302). Antinous tells Telemachus to forget about his worries over Odysseus' return and to rejoin the feast "just as before" (*Odyssey* 2.305).[26] Antinous dismisses Telemachus' words by treating him as a *hetairos* bantering about. This social dynamic meant to bully the weaker member into conformity evokes the recitation of blame poetry, which targets the poets' enemies (*ekhthroi*), but is addressed to friends (*philoi*, *hetairoi*) in convivial terms. Sometimes the target of the attack might be a companion himself, and the verbal attack a kind of admonition. An illustration of such admonition may be what Archilochus intended here: Ἐρασμονίδη Χαρίλαε, / χρῆμά τοι γελοῖον / ἐρέω, πολὺ φίλταθ' ἑταίρων, / τέρψεαι δ' ἀκούων, "Charilaus, son of Erasmon / a funny thing / I will tell you, most dearest of my *hetairoi* / and you will enjoy hearing it" (fr. 168 W). The "funny thing" could be about Charilaus himself. In this regard another of Archilochus' fragments has it thus: σὺ γὰρ δὴ παρὰ φίλων ἀπάγχεαι, "It is by your friends that you are choked" (fr. 129 W).

Yet, while in the Archilochus fragment we might expect Charilaus to join in the fun, in the *Odyssey* Telemachus declines Antinous' invitation to return to the feast because he has a different kind of communal feasting in mind, one which favors tranquility over bantering and ridiculing (*Odyssey* 2.310–317). Nevertheless, from Antinous' point of view, Telemachus behaves as a *hetairos* who cannot handle the heat of insult among friends, and thus needs to be consoled and coaxed back to the party (*Odyssey* 2.305). In a similar passage, Antinous again performs to his *hetairoi*, and mocks Odysseus disguised as beggar. He speaks derisively about Odysseus in his presence and then speaks insultingly and directly to him:

τὸν δ' αὖτ' Ἀντίνοος ἀπαμείβετο φώνησέν τε·
"τίς δαίμων τόδε πῆμα προσήγαγε, δαιτὸς ἀνίην;
στῆθ' οὕτως ἐς μέσσον, ἐμῆς ἀπάνευθε τραπέζης,
μὴ τάχα πικρὴν Αἴγυπτον καὶ Κύπρον ἵκηαι ..."

And Antinous again responded and called out to him
"What *daemon* brought forth this pain, a nuisance to our banquet?

---

[26] Telemachus is characterized as weak in that he has relented before, and even Penelope herself corroborates the charge that Telemachus is often socializing with the suitors (*Odyssey* 18.166–167).

Stand back to the middle like this, away from my table,
otherwise, you will soon come to a bitter Egypt and Cyprus."

Odyssey 17.445–448

The shifting focus between the framing narrative introducing Antinous' words (line 445), Antinous' words themselves addressed to the internal audience, the *hetairoi* (line 446), and his insulting words against the object of his attack (line 447) are clearly marked.[27] Eventually, however, Antinous, as a *kōmos* leader of sorts, goes too far, and the other suitors criticize him in turn (*Odyssey* 17.481–484). He crosses the boundary that separates the comic (*to geloion*) from the scurrilous (*to psogon*). He has brought *bōmolokhia* (abusive, excessive language and threats) to the banquet.

The word *bōmolokhia* literally means "ambush at the altar," and the related noun *bōmolokhos* means "one that lurked about the altars" to get scraps of food, like a hungry beggar (LSJ). Its metaphorical meaning would very well fit the real beggar Irus as "one who would do any dirty work to get a meal" (LSJ). One could well imagine that beggars, or indeed anyone hungry enough, would have the inclination and the impetus to fight for food. Figuratively, the word *bōmolokhia* came to mean "buffoonery" and "ribaldry" (LSJ). Indeed, the term is used in Plutarch to describe the Spartan practice called *sussitia* ("communal meals"), where the diners "had the custom of engaging in 'playful mockery' without *abuse*" (*Lycurgus* 12.4). In the case of the suitors' feasts, where mockery is pervasive, *bōmolokhia* can be harsh, or playful. In Antinous' outlandish behavior, Telemachus recognizes the suitor's desire to have all the food for himself (*Odyssey* 17.404). Thus, gluttony strips off the noble veneer among the suitors, which makes their death easier to justify.

---

[27] Concerning the smaller point of comparison between blame poetry and epic within the larger comparison between praise and blame poetry, Nagy 1979:251 observes: "As a discourse that has the capacity of telling about its subjects without necessarily speaking to them, the blame poetry of Archilochus is farther away from the praise poetry of Pindar and closer to the epic poetry of Homer." Nagy's argument is that the *iamboi* of Archilochus did not have to address Lycambes directly but in that instance were rather performed within a group (*kōmos*) of friends (*philoi*), and like epic they speak *about* their subject, whereas praise poetry is *addressed to* its subject. Taking this performance aspect into consideration (namely the role of the internal audience), the comparison I highlight here is between Archilochus' "band of friends" (*kōmos*) and Antinous' companions (*hetairoi*), for whom, and for whose benefit, he speaks. Antinous not only performs for his *hetairoi*, but also directly addresses his enemy (here the beggar). Cf. Aristotle cites Archilochus' iamb to make the point that certain things should not be spoken by certain characters, so as not to betray feelings of envy, contrariness, nor display mockery but rather "one needs to make another person say such things ... just as Archilochus deploys his *psogos* ... and makes Charon the carpenter say it in his iamb whose beginning is: 'the possessions of Gyges dripping with gold mean nothing to me'"(*Rhetoric* 1418b.42).

Nevertheless, for all the suitors' wrongfulness, the *Odyssey* and indeed Odysseus himself offer apologies for murdering them, as though the act needed expiation.[28] This apology is expressed at different points in a structured way. In the opening of the *Odyssey*, the narrative offers an apology for Odysseus' inability to save the lives of his companions "but their demise was of their own doing, because they devoured the cattle of Helios Hyperion" (*Odyssey* 1.6–9). The apology seems straightforward, but if we consider that the companions may stand for the suitors as an analogous group of young men also destroyed by Odysseus, we then see in the apology for the lost companions a prospective apology for the slaughtered suitors.[29] In fact, after the killing of the suitors, Antinous' father, Eupeithes, makes this connection explicit:

> ὦ φίλοι, ἦ μέγα ἔργον ἀνὴρ ὅδ᾽ μήσατ᾽ Ἀχαιούς.
> τοὺς μὲν σὺν νήεσσιν ἄγων πολέας τε καὶ ἐσθλούς,
> ὤλεσε μὲν νῆας γλαφυράς, ἀπὸ δ᾽ ὤλεσε λαούς,
> τοὺς δ᾽ ἐλθὼν ἔκτεινε Κεφαλλήνων ὅχ᾽ ἀρίστους

> Oh friends, truly a terrible deed has this man contrived against the
>   Achaeans,
> some together with their ships he led and destroyed, many men,
>   noble, too,
> he destroyed his hollow ships, and completely ruined his crew,
> others, on his return, he cut down, the best of the Cephallenians.

> *Odyssey* 24.426–429

The epic apologizes for the death of the suitors, because these young men are the *aristoi,* the best and noble sons of noble men (*basileis*), each from their respective cities. When Odysseus cautions the old servant Eurycleia not to boast over the dead suitors, this admonition too can be interpreted as an indirect apology.[30] Despite their execrable behavior, the punishment of the suitors is met with a certain ambivalent reaction. After all they are the *herma poléos,* the "pillar" or "mainstay" of the city (*Odyssey* 23.121). The epic solution of bringing forgetfulness and a covenant to the fathers of the slaughtered suitors in the end, in order to prevent indefinite revenge, is not the most satisfying (*Odyssey* 24.484–485).[31]

---

[28] Consider other processes of expiation by heroes, such as Heracles' twelve labors (Apollodorus *Library* 2.4.12)

[29] See Nagler 1990.

[30] Compare Archilochus: οὐ γὰρ ἐσθλὰ κατθανοῦσι κερτομεῖν ἐπ᾽ ἀνδράσι, "for it is not proper to throw insult on the dead" (134 W); cf. *Odyssey* 22.412.

[31] See Allan 2006:25n112; Danek 1998:41–42.

4

Blame and Blemish

4.1 *Mōmon Anapsai*: Internal Evidence

I have been arguing that abusive language in the *Odyssey* is connected both to the representation of blame in Greek poetry (elegiac and iambic) and in Irish satire. The language of blame and reproach in the *Odyssey* is meant to injure its victim, figuratively and, literally. In this chapter I will discuss the critical internal evidence for my proposition that blame (*mōmos*) can be read as "blemishes."[1] At *Odyssey* 2.86 we find the verbal phrase *mōmon anapsai*, defined in Liddell and Scott (LSJ) as "to set a brand." The verse contains the single occurrence of this phrase in Homer, and the word *mōmos* is a *hapax legomenon*.[2]

In response to Telemachus' charges against the suitors (*Odyssey* 2.40–79), Antinous accuses Odysseus' son of "shaming" them (*aiskhunōn*) and of attempting to "fix the blame" on them (*mōmon anapsai*), thus causing physical blemishes as I propose:

Τηλέμαχ' ὑψαγόρη, μένος[3] ἄσχετε, ποῖον ἔειπες
ἡμέας <u>αἰσχύνων</u>, ἐθέλοις δέ κε <u>μῶμον ἀνάψαι</u>·

---

[1] In this respect, it is interesting to read the following formulation by Finley 2002:125: "What tends to confuse us is the fact that the heroic world was unable to visualize any achievement or relationship except in concrete terms. The gods were anthropomorphized, the emotions and feelings were located in specific organs of the body, even the soul was materialized. Every quality or state had to be translated into some specific symbol, honor into trophy, friendship into treasure, marriage into gifts of cattle." I do subscribe to Finley's formulation and add "blemishes" as the concrete manifestation of blame. In this view, language is material, a phonological phenomenon conceived and shaped by the mouth of the poet whose intent is to cast out the blemished leader.

[2] On the matter of *hapax legomena*, it is instructive to remember that the traditional treatment of the Alexandrian scholars was not to suspect singular occurrences of words and phrases as possible manipulations of the text, but rather to distinguish which were Homeric and which were not. For the latter, Aristarchus used the *obelus* (*mōmos* was not marked), and for the former he states the following (preserved in Aristonicus in Scholia A Γ 54): "there are many *hapax legomena* in the poet's work" (Pfeiffer 1968, 1998:229). See also Martinazzoli 1957.

[3] In Liddell and Scott's Greek lexicon, *menos* is translated as "might," "force," "strength," "spirit," or "passion." In this passage, it would not make sense for Antinous to be praising Telemachus for his "strength" or other related meanings. In fact, Antinous is mocking Telemachus' impetus

σοὶ δ' οὔ τι μνηστῆρες Ἀχαιῶν αἴτιοί εἰσιν,
ἀλλὰ φίλη μήτηρ, ἥ τοι πέρι κέρδεα οἶδεν.

Telemachus, you big/fancy talker, you are impetuous,[4] saying this
  sort of thing,
<u>shaming</u> us, you wish you could <u>fasten the blame/blemish</u> on us.
However, for your information, the Achaean suitors are not guilty
rather, it is your dear mother because she knows how to take
  advantage.

Odyssey 2.85–88

Antinous mockingly addresses Telemachus, calling him a "big and fancy talker"
(*hupsagorē*),[5] in response to the young man's public criticism of the suitors in the
assembly. Antinous rebukes Telemachus for attempting to "fasten blemish" on
them, *mōmon anapsai* (μῶμον ἀνάψαι). In the analysis of this phrase, I will take a
closer look at the verb *anapsai* (*an-haptō*). The verbs *anaptō* (*an-haptō*) and *haptō*
are related, but are presented in two separate entries in the *Greek-English Lexicon*
(LSJ). The entry for *haptō* gives "fasten or bind to," as in "fastening the string
for the lyre" (*Odyssey* 21.408); the entry for *anaptō* shows "make fast on, or to."
Importantly, *anaptō*, as distinct from *haptō*, occurs only in the *Odyssey*: ἀνάψαι
(*Odyssey* 2.86), ἀνῆπτον (*Odyssey* 12.179), ἀνήφθω (*Odyssey* 12.51, 162). Under
the entry for *mōmon*, the LSJ cites the example at *Odyssey* 2.86 and defines the
phrase *mōmon anapsai* as "to set a brand," evocative of both figurative ("fasten
reproach") and literal meanings such as "fastening ropes on a mast" at *Odyssey*
12.179 (ὀρθὸν ἐν ἱστοπέδῃ, ἐκ δ' αὐτοῦ πείρατ' ἀνῆπτον).

---

to criticize the suitors at the assembly (*Odyssey* 2.40–79). Antinous intends it as a backhanded
compliment. He acknowledges Telemachus' *menos* so that he can challenge and then dismiss it.
In this regard, I find the distinction between the two kinds of *menos* given in Doederlein 1850: 91
relevant, as one kind refers to an aggressive stance ("boldness"), while the other to a passive one
("persistence," from the verb "to stay" [*menein*]): "Die Lust, der Wille, ist homonym mit μένος
die Ausdauer, von ménein, bleiben ... Beide Begriffe begegnen sich in dem Begriff der Kraft, aber
unterscheiden sich als offensive und als defensive Äusserung der Kraft, wie impetus oder *vis* und
constantia," "Desire, the will, is homonymous with μένος the perseverance, from *menein*, stay ...
Both terms converge with the power, but differ as offensive and defensive expressions of power,
such as impetus or *vis* and *constantia*." I think Antinous ridicules Telemachus for both aspects of
menos: "attack" or "force," as well as his "persistence" in laying the blame on them.

4   In this passage I settled for "impetuous" as a translation for *menos*, despite its other meaning,
"persistence" or "constantia" (see note 3 above), because Antinous still has in mind Telemachus'
address at the assembly, which was a form of attack (*impetus*).

5   For an interpretation of *hupsagorē* in a positive sense as "well spoken," see the brief discussion on
Odysseus among the Phaeacians and the theme of "instruction of princes" in Chapter 4, Section
6. In addition, I point to the overt contrast between "high" (the *hupsos* part of the compound
word) and "low" (blame and shame).

There is no significant difference between *anaptō* and *haptō*, but the preposition *ana* ("on," "onto," "upon," "along") when in composition (e.g. *anabainō,* to go up) includes the sense of repetition, increase, and completion, an action done again and again (e.g. *Iliad* 18.562 and *Odyssey* 24.343). Therefore, both *haptō* and *anaptō* are predominantly used with a literal meaning such as "to make fast stern cables" (πρυμνήσι ἀνάψαι, *Odyssey* 9.137), "to touch" or "to take" food (σίτου θ' ἅπτεσθον, *Odyssey* 4.60), "to be set on fire," as in "the olive wood was about / to touch the fire" (ὁ μοχλὸς ἐλάϊνος ἐν πυρὶ μέλλεν / ἅψεσθαι, *Odyssey* 9.378–379), among others.[6] Consider Telemachus' words about Odysseus as beggar: ξεῖνος ὅδ᾽· οὐ γὰρ ἀεργὸν ἀνέξομαι ὅς κεν ἐμῆς γε / χοίνικος,[7] ἅπτηται καὶ τηλόθεν εἰληλουθώς, "This stranger here, I will not allow anyone to be idle, who touches my / portion of meal, even if he comes from afar" (*Odyssey* 19.27–28).

An example of *haptō* particularly suited for the context of blame, encompassing both the physical and figurative denotations, is found at *Odyssey* 22.41: νῦν ὑμῖν καὶ πᾶσιν ὀλέθρου πείρατ᾽ ἐφῆπται, "now the ropes of destruction are fastened upon all of you." The context for these threatening words is the impending obliteration of the suitors at Odysseus' hands. The threat is a fitting response to Antinous' protestation at *Odyssey* 2.86: ἐθέλοις δέ κε μῶμον ἀνάψαι, "you wish you could fasten the blemish on us." Thus, *olethrou peirat' ephēptai* is semantically and structurally analogous to *mōmon anapsai* and a response to it. To put it differently, Antinous says, "You wish you could fasten blemishes on us," and in book 22 Odysseus responds, "Yes, the ropes of destruction will be fastened on you." The call and response highlights the relationship between these two phrases and the intersection between the literal and the figurative uses of *haptō* and its compounds. The two expressions paraphrase each other in that the encoded physical aspect of *mōmon anapsai* is made explicit in *olethrou peirat' ephēptai*. In other words, the critical issue is that *mōmon anapsai* is negative criticism which can lead to physical punishment. A particularly remarkable definition of *haptō*, which emphasizes *mōmos* as blemish, is given in Bauer's Lexikon:[8] "to cause illuminatio n or burning to take place." From this, I also read "burning" as "inflammation" or "redness" on the skin.

---

[6] For further examples of *haptō*, see also *Iliad* 1.512, 2.152, 8.339, 10.377; *Odyssey* 3.274 ("to hang up," as in offerings in a temple), Pindar *Nemean* 8.22; Aeschylus *Agamemnon* 1608 ("fasten upon"); Thucydides 2.50 ("to feed in human flesh"); Aristophanes *Frogs* 255 and 572; Plato *Ion* 535a3 ("to touch," "to affect"). For further examples of *anaptō*, see Euripides *Andromache* 1196 ("to attach"); Herodotus 2.133; Plato *Timaeus* 39b line 4 ("to kindle").

[7] *Khoinikos* (*khoinix*): a dry measure, about a quart (for example, of corn). It was one man's daily allowance (LSJ).

[8] A Greek-English lexicon of the New Testament, and other early Christian literature (1971:533).

Elsewhere in Homer the use of *haptō* corroborates the literal and physical aspect of *mōmon anapsai*. In both the *Iliad* and the *Odyssey*, *haptō* almost always signifies physical action, the most frequent and conventional of which is a suppliant's gesture of clasping the knees of the person or divinity being supplicated. For example, Thetis clasps Zeus' knees, Θέτις δ᾽ ὡς ἥψατο γούνων (*Iliad* 1.512). The same supplicating gesture occurs in various other passages, always with the verb *haptō* (*Iliad* 4.357, 15.76, 20.468, and 21.65). In the *Odyssey* we also find this conventional gesture of supplication in various scenes (*Odyssey* 6.169, 19.473, 22.339). In addition to the "clasping of the knees," virtually all other instances of *haptō* and *anaptō* in Homer have a physical connotation, for example there is πρυμνήσι᾽ ἀνάψαι, "to fasten stern cables" (*Odyssey* 9.137), and ἐκ δ᾽αὐτοῦ [ἱστοῦ] πείρατ᾽ ἀνήφθω, "let the ropes be fastened on the ends of it [mast]" (*Odyssey* 12.50–51, 178-179).

The evidence shows that *haptō* and *anaptō* are almost always used in a physical sense in Homeric poetry,[9] and therefore *mōmon anapsai* conveys physical meaning alongside its figurative sense afforded by the conventional translation of *mōmos* as "blame" rather than "blemish." The two meanings "blame" and "blemish" work as a wordplay. Notably, another *haptō* compound *pros-haptō* ("to attach," "bestow") in its variant *protiaptō* at *Iliad* 24.110 is used to express praise when paired with *kudos* ("renown," "honor," and "glory," especially in war): αὐτὰρ ἐγὼ τόδε κῦδος Ἀχιλλῆϊ προτιάπτω, "but I bestow this *kudos* on Achilles." Thus, I suggest that *kudos protiaptō* represents a Homeric expression of praise, while *mōmon anaptō* an expression of blame.[10]

Grammatically the verb *haptō* requires both direct and indirect objects (fixing something on someone). In our phrase *mōmon anapsai*, the dative *hēmin* ("onto/against us") is elided, but inferred from *hēmeas* (*hēmeas aiskhunōn*) in the first half of the verse. Not only is *hēmin* to be understood from *hēmeas*, but so too is *aiskhunōn* ("to disfigure," "to make ugly"), a reflection of *mōmon anapsai*. As I have just illustrated, the verb *haptō*, even with different prefixes (*ana, pros, epi*), still maintains its essentially physical meaning of "fixing" a thing onto another, whether we are speaking about "blemishes" (*Odyssey* 2.86), "cables" (*Odyssey* 9.13), or "ropes of destruction" (*Odyssey* 22.41). Outside Homer, we find a relevant example in Menander fr.1083.4. A character is blaming another for his lack

---

[9]   Outside Homer we find the figurative meaning of *haptō* in Sophocles' *Oedipus at Colonus* 236. Here *pros-haptō* is used with the word "debt" (*khreos*): μή τι πέρα χρέος / ἐμᾷ πόλει προσάψῃς, "lest you fix (charge) even more debt to my city."

[10] In Pindar we find *pros-haptō* in a phrase which is the opposite of *kudos protiaptō*: μὴ τὸ δύσφαμον προσάψω, "may I not attach infamy" (*Nemean* 8. 37). Note the difference between the neuter noun κῦδος "praise" (with the circumflex accent), and the masculine noun κύδος "reproach," "abuse" (with an acute accent), hence the verb κυδάζω (Sophocles *Ajax* 722: <u>κυδάζεται</u> τοῖς πᾶσιν Ἀργείοις ὁμοῦ, "he [Teucer] is reviled by all the Argives").

of courage in carrying out a task: "you fix/assign (*prosaptei*)[11] the responsibility/ the cause (*aitian*) to fortune (*tukhēi*)." In a fragment of Sophocles (fr. 257 Jebb, Headlam[12]), we find the expression *mōmos hapsetai*, the closest ancient example to the Homeric *mōmon anapsai*: ὡς νῦν τάχος στείχωμεν. οὐ γὰρ ἔσθ᾽ ὅπως / σπουδῆς δικαίας μῶμος ἄψεται ποτε, "now let us follow speedily; there is no way *mōmos* will cling to just haste."[13] And in Pindar, we see a variation in diction: μῶμος ... κρέμαται ("blame that hangs," *Olympian* 6.74).

In Pindar's *Nemean 8*, the poet contrasts the character (*ethos*) of praise and blame poets through imagery, and diction that are physical in nature:

πολλὰ γὰρ πολλᾷ λέλεκται· νεαρὰ δ᾽ ἐξευρόντα δόμεν βασάνῳ
ἐς ἔλεγχον, ἅπας κίνδυνος· ὄψον δὲ λόγοι φθονεροῖσιν·
ἅπτεται δ᾽ ἐσλῶν ἀεί, χειρόνεσσι δ᾽οὐκ ἐρίζει.
κεῖνος καὶ Τελαμῶνος δάψεν υἱὸν φασγάνῳ ἀμφικυλίσαις.
ἦ τιν᾽ ἄγλωσσον μέν, ἦτορ δ᾽ ἄλκιμον, λάθα κατέχει
ἐν λυγρῷ νείκει . . .

Many stories have been told in many ways. But to put newly found
        things to the test
of genuiness is all danger. Words are a treat for the envious;
and envy <u>always fastens onto the noble</u>,[14] but against the ignoble it
        does not quarrel.
That envy even devoured the son of Telamon [Ajax] with the twisting
        of his own sword.
A man, not gifted in speech,[15] but strong in his heart, subdued by
        oblivion
mournful strife ...

---

11 As a philosophical and technical term, *pros-haptō* means "to apply" a concept or analogy to something: ταύτην τοίνυν, ἦν δ᾽ ἐγώ, τὴν εἰκόνα, ὦ φίλε Γλαύκων, προσαπτέον ἅπασαν τοῖς ἔμπροσθεν λεγομένοις, " 'Thus,' I said, 'this image, dear Glaucon, must be applied as a whole to what has been discussed above' " (Plato *Republic* 7.517b 1).

12 Cambridge 1917:193.

13 Albeit late evidence (fourth century CE), the phrase *mōmos haptetai* appears in Gregory of Nazianzus, the *Theologian* 1205.6-7: Καὶ τοῦτ᾽ ἀφήσω, τὴν χάριν δόξῃ κρατεῖν / Πάντες τεθήπασί σ᾽, οὐδ᾽ ὁ μῶμος ἅπτεται., "And I will say this, that grace rules over reputation, everyone is amazed at you, and blame does not cling to you."

14 Envy "<u>fastens</u> criticism onto" the nobles, but it does not quarrel with the <u>base</u>," ἅπτεται δ᾽ ἐσλῶν ἀεί, <u>χειρόνεσσι</u> δ᾽ οὐκ ἐρίζει. Significantly, Pindar's representation of abusive language also fits the characterization of Thersites, whose ethos is to criticize kings (*erizemenai basileusin*, *Iliad* 2.214). See Kouklanakis 1999 for an analysis of Thersites' speech.

15 Ajax is the only other character described in this way in Homer, besides Thersites and Telemachus. However, with Ajax we find the redeeming quality of the hero's "brave heart," and exceptional prowess in battle.

The power of abusive language in this poem is formulated in terms of physical violence and death: *haptetai* ("fasten onto"), *dapsen* ("devour"), *phasganōi amphikulisais* ("twisting on one's own sword"), amid *lugrōi neikei* ("sorrowful quarrel"). Furthermore, Pindar presents blame speech as "misrepresentation," deceitful talk, and "damaging reproach":

> ... ἐχθρὰ δ' ἄρα πάρφασις ἦν καὶ πάλαι,
> αἱμύλων μύθων ὁμόφοιτος, δολοφραδής, κακοποιὸν ὄνειδος·
> ἃ τὸ μὲν λαμπρὸν βιᾶται, τῶν δ' ἀφάντων κῦδος ἀντείνει σαθρόν.
> εἴη μή ποτέ μοι τοιοῦτον ἦθος, Ζεῦ πάτερ, ἀλλὰ κελεύθοις
> ἁπλόαις ζωᾶς ἐφαπτοίμαν, θανὼν ὡς παισὶ κλέος
> μὴ τὸ δύσφαμον προσάψω. χρυσὸν εὔχονται, πεδίον δ' ἕτεροι
> ἀπέραντον· ἐγὼ δ' ἀστοῖς ἁδὼν καὶ χθονὶ γυῖα καλύψω
> αἰνέων αἰνητά, μομφὰν δ' ἐπισπείρων ἀλιτροῖς.

> Yet, <u>hateful misrepresentation</u> is old: a companion of flattering tales,
>   deceitful, and <u>reproachful evildoing</u> disgrace. She uses force
>   against illustrious men, but extends <u>rotten glory</u> to those
>   who do not shine. May I never have such a <u>character/nature</u>,
>   father Zeus; may I <u>cling to</u> clean paths of life, so that upon
>   dying I shall <u>cast glory</u> on my children,
> not <u>infamy</u>. Some men pray for gold, others for boundless land; but
>   I, pleasing my fellow-citizens, wish my limbs to be buried in
>   the earth
> by <u>praising the praiseworthy</u>, and <u>sowing blame (momphan) on the</u>
>   <u>shameful</u>.

Pindar Nemean 8.20–39

Unlike the suitors, Pindar prays to Zeus so that he may *cling* to the "clean paths of life," and not *fasten* "infamy" or "ill-fame" onto his children. The poet's wish, though expressed as a personal prayer, serves as a general admonition, an *ainos*: "do not wish to be such a type/of such character (*toiouton ēthos*)." In the end those who have such character (infamous, blameworthy) will have "blame" (*momphan*)[16] from better men. Thus, both "to cast glory, not infamy" (*kleos mē to dusphamon prosapto* lines 36-37) and "sowing reproach (*momphan epispeirōn*,"

---

[16] The LSJ gives *hē momphē* ("blame," "reproof") as the poetic form of *hē mempsis*. An interesting citation comes from Euripides' *Alcestis* 1007–1008: φίλον πρὸς ἄνδρα χρὴ λέγειν ἐλευθέρως, Ἄδμητε, μομφὰς δ' οὐχ ὑπὸ σπλάγχνοις ἔχειν, "to a friend one must speak freely, / Admetus, not to hold blame in his heart." The form *mempsis* (cross-referenced under *ho momphos*) is glossed as *duskleia*, "ill-fame" or "infamy."

line 39) are analogous to Antinous' *mōmon anapsai* in content and diction, but only *mōmon anapsai* conveys the notion of physically injurious words which may result in blemishes on the skin, akin to Irish satire. Finally, the implication of the various aspects of blame language is summed up in the last verse (line 39), which elegantly and skillfully articulates the essential paradigm: "praising the praiseworthy" and "sowing blame on the shameful," αἰνέων αἰνητά, μομφὰν δ' ἐπισπείρων ἀλιτροῖς.

As I mentioned above, the Homeric articulation of this paradigmatic opposition in Pindar can be summed up by the contrast between *kudos protiaptō* ("bestowing *kudos*")[17] and *mōmon anapsai* ("fastening blemishes"). In this opposition in poetry and in ideology (as we can assume elite bias in Pindar similar to what we see in Aristotle), praise is the realm of the noble, and blame of the base. But to a discernible and significant extent, the *Odyssey* complicates these polarities, if not the aesthetics, of praise and blame. The suitors' speeches have the social and political function to disqualify Telemachus based on his shortcomings and to gain kingship through marriage at all cost, including killing Telemachus (*Odyssey* 22.53). Here too their speech can be analogized to the social and juridical function of Irish satire.

Furthermore, in its middle form, *haptomai* means to "kill oneself by hanging" (LSJ). In his journey to the underworld Odysseus learns about Oedipus' mother: ἀψαμένη βρόχον αἰπὺν ἀφ' ὑψηλοῖο μελάθρου, "and she [Epicaste] went to Hades ... after hanging [herself] on a high noose from a lofty roof" (*Odyssey* 11.278). In addition, *anaptō* has the more specialized meaning of "hang [something] up" as *agalmata* (temple offerings), similar to the verb *anatithēmi* ("set up"). For example, Aegisthus "hangs sacrifices up" at the sacred altars of the gods following his killing of Agamemnon:

> πολλὰ δὲ μηρία κῆε θεῶν ἱεροῖς ἐπὶ βωμοῖς,
> πολλὰ δ' ἀγάλματ' ἀνῆψεν, ὑφάσματά τε χρυσόν τε,
> ἐκτελέσας μέγα ἔργον, ὃ οὔ ποτε ἔλπετο θυμῷ.

> And many thigh pieces did he set afire at the holy altars of the gods,
> and many offerings he hung up, woven and golden objects,
> for the accomplishment of a terrible deed, which he never hoped for
>   in his heart.

> *Odyssey* 3.274–276

---

[17] See Detienne 1973:21 for a discussion of the contrast between *kudos* and *kleos*.

Further exploration of *haptō* alongside two cognate nouns reinforces the physical meaning of the verb. These cognate nouns are homonyms and are differentiated only by their accents. The first is ἁψίς (*hapsis,* genitive: *hapsidos*) from *haptō,* a feminine noun with accent on the ultima, and it means "loop" or "mesh" (*Iliad* 5.487),[18] "felloe of a wheel" (Hesiod *Works and Days* 426), "wheel" (Euripides *Hippolytus* 1233), and "potter's wheel" (*Greek Anthology* 4.191). There is also a metaphorical sense "to bend the wheels of words," *kamptei epōn hapsidas* (Aristophanes *Thesmophoriazusae* 53). The second cognate, ἅψις (*hápsis,* genitive: *hapseos,* and *-ios* in Ionic), a feminine noun related to *haptomai,* means "touching" and "contact;" it is also used in medicine to describe "distraction of the mind," *hapsis phrenōn* (Hippocrates *On Acute Diseases* 52). Penelope's own bending of words and distracting of the suitors' minds become the suitors' version and justification for their outlandish behavior: "to all she gives hope and makes promises to each man / sending messages, but her mind *contrives* other things" (*Odyssey* 2.91–95). Weaving becomes a mimetic representation of her deception: "thus for three years she eluded and convinced the Achaeans with her craft (*dolōi*)" (*Odyssey* 2.106).[19] It is in Antinous' rebuke against Telemachus that we first encounter the story of Penelope's weaving in Homer (2. 94–100).[20] Indeed, Penelope's weaving is meant precisely to distract the suitors' minds. Her crafty and handy work is at once malicious deception and extraordinary cleverness (*Odyssey* 2.115–121). Therefore, both *hapsís* and *hápsis* in their literal and figurative meanings—a "wheel," "distraction of mind," "weaving," and "craftiness"— offer interesting corollaries for *mōmon anapsai* when understood as the power of (poetic and prophetic) words to affect reality.

To sum up, the physical connotation of *haptō* and *anaptō* is critical for my proposition that *mōmon anapsai* is coded language for physical blemishing. The verb activates the literal meaning of *mōmos* as "blemish" (which I will discuss in more detail in Chapter 4, Section 3) and expands the range of interpretation beyond the conceptual "blame" or "reproach." As I have mentioned above, one of the definitions given for *mōmon anapsai* is "to set a brand,"[21] which, though denoting a physical phenomenon, lacks the magical dimension caused by injurious words. It is this critical interpretation of *mōmon anapsai* at *Odyssey* 2.86

---

[18] In epic and Ionic dialects, the form is written with smooth breathing mark, without aspiration (*h*-sound): ἀψίς, not ἁψίς.

[19] Compare *huphainō* (weaving) as "contriving": *Odyssey* 4.678, 5.356, 9.422; *Iliad* 3.212, 6.187.

[20] Compare Penelope weaving in Plato's *Phaedo* (84a6).

[21] Cf. Latin *notare,* which has the same meaning. See Horace *Satire* 1.4.1-5: Eupolis atque Cratinus Aristophanesque poetae / atque alii, quorum comoedia prisca virorum est, / si quis erat dignus describi, quod malus ac fur, / quod moechus foret aut sicarius aut alioqui / famosus, multa cum libertate notabant.

that establishes the contrast between Homeric blame poetics in the *Odyssey* and the Irish poetic tradition of blame conceived as blemishes induced by "satire," that is, injurious words. Whereas in the Irish tradition satire against kings has the explicit purpose of belittling, hence disqualifying the ruler, in the *Odyssey* this purpose is encoded and implicit. It operates through the superiority of epic praise, that is, the inherent praiseworthiness of Odysseus, the true hero-king in contrast to the blameworthiness of the suitors (those who lack kingship and heroic status).[22] Moreover, as I will show, outside the *Odyssey* there is Greek evidence for a more explicit link between criticism of kings and physical blemishes.

4.2 *Mōmos* and *Mōlōps*: The Greek Evidence for Satirical Poets and Blemished Kings

I now turn to a closer examination of the word *mōmos* itself ("blame," "reproach," and "disgrace"). The LSJ offers the meaning "blame" and cites *Odyssey* 2.86 as the critical evidence.[23] The premier and only evidence for *mōmos* as "blemish" (to be distinguished from "blame," "reproach," or "disgrace") comes from the *Septuagint* Leviticus 24.19: καὶ ἐάν τις δῷ <u>μῶμον</u> τῷ πλησίον ὡς ἐποίησεν αὐτῷ, ὡσαύτως ἀντιποιηθήσεται αὐτῷ, "If anyone should 'cause a <u>blemish</u>' ('injure') on his neighbor, just as he has done, it shall be done onto him."[24] This later

---

[22] As an example of such a concept, Nausicaa's suitors in Alcinous' court (Book 8) are also competing for kingship, but they reveal themselves unsuitable for the role, especially Euryalus who taunts Odysseus with ill-chosen words. Likewise, Penelope's suitors cannot fit the role of *basileus* because of their execrable behavior.

[23] Other evidence cited are Semonides 7.84, 105; Pindar *Olympian* 6.74, *Pythian* 1.82; Bacchylides 12.202; *Greek Anthology* 4.84; Sophocles fr. 257; Cambridge 1917:193; *Septuagint* Sirach 11.31; Cicero *Letters to Atticus* 5.20.6; Plutarch *Praecepta gerenda reipublicae* 2.820a; and Lucian *Hermotimus*. In Herodianus' *Epimerismoi*, *mōmos* is glossed as *ho psogos*, "blame," "reproach." In Plutarch *Praecepta* 2.820a we find the following: ὥσπερ οὖν ὁ Πλάτων ἀκουστέον εἶναι τοῖς νέοις ἔλεγεν ἐκ παίδων εὐθύς, ὡς οὔτε περικεῖσθαι χρυσὸν αὐτοῖς ἔξωθεν οὔτε κεκτῆσθαι θέμις, οἰκεῖον ἐν τῇ ψυχῇ συμμεμιγμένον ἔχοντας, αἰνιττόμενος οἶμαι τὴν ἐκ γένους διατείνουσαν εἰς τὰς φύσεις αὐτῶν ἀρετήν· οὕτω παραμυθώμεθα τὴν φιλοτιμίαν, λέγοντες ἐν ἑαυτοῖς ἔχειν χρυσὸν ἀδιάφθορον καὶ ἀκήρατον καὶ ἄχραντον <u>ὑπὸ φθόνου καὶ μώμου τιμήν</u>, ἅμα λογισμῷ καὶ παραθεωρήσει τῶν πεπραγμένων ἡμῖν καὶ πεπολιτευμένων, "Therefore, just as Plato said that young people should be told from childhood that it is not proper for them to wear gold on their persons or to possess it, since they have a gold of their own mingled in their souls,—a figurative reference, I believe, to the virtue derived by descent, which permeates their natures,—so let us moderate our ambition, saying that we have in ourselves honour, a gold uncorrupted, undefiled, and unpolluted by <u>envy and fault-finding</u>, which increases along with reasoning and the contemplation of our acts and public measures" (translated by Fowler 1936).

[24] For other instances of *mōmos* as "blemish" relating to sacrificial victims see also *Septuagint* Deuteronomy 15.21 and 17.1, concerning the practice of sacrifices. The details on the propriety and requirements for the sacrificial victims are specified in Leviticus 22.18–25. In the New

meaning of *mōmos* in the *Septuagint* is already encoded in the Homeric evidence at *Odyssey* 2.86. The word is also used in the context of animal sacrifice. Indeed, we find the following elaboration on the rules for animal sacrifice in Philo (first century BCE):

> And all [animal victims] must be whole, *with no sickness* (*kērainonta*) on any part of their bodies, entirely *undamaged* (*asinē*) in every part, *free of blemish* (*mōmōn ametokha*). At all events, so great is the caution used with respect not only to those who lead the sacrifices, but also to the victims which are offered, that the most eminent of the priests are carefully selected for examining *blemishes* (*mōmōn*), and they scrutinize them [victims] from head to foot, both the parts which are visible and those which are hidden, such as the belly and the thighs, lest any slight imperfection (*lōbē*) should escape notice. And the accuracy and minuteness of the investigation is directed not so much on account of the victims themselves, but in order that those who offer them should be *blameless* (*anupaitiou*); for he [God] wishes to teach them [Jews] by these signs, whenever they approach the altars or pray or give thanks, never to bring with them any weakness or sickness or passion in their soul, but to ensure to make it [the soul] entirely *flawless* (*akēlidōton*), so that God might not turn away from the sight of it. [25]

> Philo *On Special Laws* 1.34

In the passage above we note that Philo's word for "blameless," when used for people, is *anupaitiou* (from *aitia*). In book 1.5, Philo starts by explaining the superiority of male animals over female animals for the purpose of sacrifice. Philo extends his discussion toward the notion that the male human is more perfect (*teleioteron*) than the female, but only if he is "blemish-free" (*amōmos*). In his examination of the best qualities of the sacrificial victim itself ("whole animal" [*holokautos*]), Philo cannot help establishing an analogy between the wholeness

---

Testament we find the same meaning of "blemish" in 2 Peter 2: concerning the profane and the blasphemous: οὗτοι δέ, ὡς ἄλογα ζῷα γεγεννημένα φυσικὰ εἰς ἅλωσιν καὶ φθοράν, ἐν οἷς ἀγνοοῦσιν βλασφημοῦντες, ἐν τῇ φθορᾷ αὐτῶν καὶ φθαρήσονται· ἀδικούμενοι μισθὸν ἀδικίας. ἡδονὴν ἡγούμενοι τὴν ἐν ἡμέρᾳ τρυφήν, σπίλοι καὶ μῶμοι ἐντρυφῶντες ἐν ταῖς ἀπάταις αὐτῶν συνευωχούμενοι ὑμῖν, "But these as natural brute beasts, made to be taken and destroyed, speak evil of the things that they understand not; and shall utterly perish in their own corruption; And shall receive the reward of unrighteousness, as they that count it pleasure to riot in the daytime. Spots they are and blemishes, sporting themselves with their own deceivings while they feast with you" (2 Peter 2.12-13 King James).

[25] I have adapted Colson's 1937 translation based on the critical edition by Cohn and Wendland (1906).

(*teleias*) of an animal "free of blemish" (*mōmōn ametokha*) in the first passage and the "wholeness" of a man who is "free of blemish" (*hos amōmos*) in the second passage:[26]

> And then let the whole victim be given to the fire of the altar of God, having become one from many parts, and from the many, one. These things, then, are understood in express words of command. But another meaning is revealed, which has an enigmatic expression through signs, and the words spoken are the visible symbols of the unknown (*adēlōn*)[27] and the invisible. Now the victim which is to be sacrificed as a whole burnt offering must be a male, because a male, compared to the female, is *more perfect* (*teleioteron*), more prone to leadership, and nearly related to the efficient cause; for the female is *imperfect* (*ateles*), submissive, and proven to be more given to suffer action than to act. And since the elements of which our soul consists are two in number, the rational and the irrational parts, *the rational part belongs to the male sex*, which has been endowed with mind and reason; but the irrational part belongs to the sex of woman, that which endows the senses. And the mind is superior to the senses as the man is to the woman in every respect, who, *free of blemish* [*hos amōmos*] and purified with the proper purifications, namely, the perfect virtues (*tais aretēs teleias*), becomes himself the most holy sacrifice, being wholly and in all respects pleasing to God.[28]

Philo *On Special Laws* 1.5

In the *Dictionnaire d'etymologie de la langue Grecque*, Chantraine explains the phonology of the conventional honorific title *amumōn*, relating it to *mōmos*. Therefore the early meaning of *amumōn* was most likely "faultless, unblemished, without physical defect," and it must have been related to the requirement that a *basileus* be unblemished in order to rule, that is, with no physical

---

[26] Cf. Hesiod's *amōmos*, "blemish-free," in human terms as a reference to physical beauty (*Theogony* 258–260): Πουλυνόη τε καὶ Αὐτονόη καὶ Λυσιάνασσα / Εὐάρνη τε φυὴν ἐρατὴ καὶ <u>εἶδος ἄμωμος</u>, "Polynoe, and Autonoe, and Lysianassa, / Euarne, lovely of shape and without <u>blemish of form</u>."

[27] I will discuss the word *adēlōn* below in Chapter 4, Section 3 in connection to burnt sacrifice.

[28] Compare Bartelink 1960:44: "Bei Philo wird ἄμωμος sowohl von der kultischen Makellosigkeit des Opfertieres (wofür man im klassischen Griechisch die Adjektiva *holoklēros* und *teleios* verwendete) wie von der Tadellosigkeit der Frommen vor Gott gebraucht)," "In the case of Philo, ἄμωμος is used both for the sacrificial animal (for which the adjectives *holoklēros* and *teleios* were used in classical Greek) and for the impeccability of the pious before God." Thus, while in Philo both animals and man must be *amōmos*, *holoklēros*, and *teleios* ("blameless," "whole," and "perfect") in their own attributes (physical perfection and virtues respectively), in the Homeric world the animal to be sacrificed must be perfect, unlike humans whose imperfections (*mōmos*) can lead to their sacrifice.

defect, perhaps even handsome.[29] While in Homer we find *teleios* for a "blemish-free" sacrificial victim, *basileōs amumonos* (*Odyssey* 19.109) is the attribute for a "blemish-free" king. To the extent that kings were in charge of ritual sacrifices, Philo's use of the words *mōmos* and *amōmos*, however late the evidence, shows the same contours attested in Chantraine, and supports my argument that the suitors are disqualified to become kings because they have been blamed and blemished in poetry by virtually every character.

Therefore, when Antinous repudiates Telemachus' reproaches, he articulates a dominant concern of the suitors, namely, to avoid being "blemished," thus disqualified from the title *amumōn basileus* of Ithaca. Thus, *mōmos*, alongside other words of insult—*lōbē* ("outrage"), *oneidea* ("insults"), *elenkheia* ("talk of the people"), *kertomia* ("criticism")—belongs to diction that represents blame poetry, and when idiomatically coupled with *anaptō*, it expresses its physical dimension. While the verb forms *memphomai, mōmeuō / mōmaomai / mōmeomai*[30] are near synonyms with *mōmon anapsai*,[31] only the verbal phrase *mōmon anapsai* expresses the physical manifestation of the insult.

The critical Greek evidence supporting the physical interpretation of *mōmon anapsai* is found in Strabo (14.1.39), an explicit illustration of the connection between poetic satire and kingship. In his observations about the region inhabited by the Magnesians, Strabo mentions Daphitas,[32] a *grammatikos*,[33] learned man, and poet, who is said to have been put to death because he mocked (*loidorēsanta*) the kings of Magnesia with a distich:[34]

κεῖται δ' ἐν πεδίῳ πρὸς ὄρει καλουμένῳ Θώρακι ἡ πόλις, ἐφ' ᾧ σταυρωθῆναί φασι Δαφίταν τὸν γραμματικὸν <u>λοιδορήσαντα τοὺς</u> <u>βασιλέας διὰ διστίχου·</u>

---

[29] Compare Plato, *Laws* 6.759c: Kings should be ὁλόκληρον καὶ γνήσιον, "wholesome and noble." Cf. *The Battle of Magh Tuireadh*: King Bres's predecessor, King Nuada, had lost his hand in combat, and was forced out of kingship by a divine decree that a maimed king could not rule.

[30] See Parry 1973:29–38, especially chapter 2, where the author gives a useful survey of *mōmos* and its related verb in Homer and in other authors.

[31] All three forms of the verb are transitive and admit both accusative and dative, depending on whether the semantic stress is on "assigning blame" or "finding fault."

[32] In Brill's *New Pauly*, the entry for Daphitas (Montanari 2006) is as follows: "Greek grammarian ('sophist,' according to Val. Max. 1, 8), probably from the 2nd cent. BC, if it is accepted that he lived at the same time as Attalus III. The *Suda* (δ 99 s.v. Δαφίδας, 'Daphidas') says that he came from Telmessus in Caria and made claims about Homer, saying that the poet was not telling the truth because the Athenians did not take part in the expedition to Troy."

[33] In the *Suda's* entry for Antimachus of Colophonian, the attribution *grammatikos* is coupled with *poiētēs*: Ἀντίμαχος Κολοφώνιος, υἱὸς Ὑπάρχου, γραμματικὸς καὶ ποιητής, "Antimachus of Colophon, son of Hyparchus, the grammarian and poet."

[34] A *distikhos* means "doubly woven," that is, a couplet (LSJ), akin to the Irish *glam dicend*, or couplet *décoché*.

πορφύρεοι μώλωπες, ἀπορρινήματα γάζης
Λυσιμάχου, Λυδῶν ἄρχετε καὶ Φρυγίης."

On the plain near the mountain called Thorax lies the city in which they say that Daphitas was crucified, the grammarian [poet/scholar] who had mocked the kings with a distich:
  "Purple stripes, filings of the treasure
  of Lysimachus, you rule over the Lydians and Phrygians."

Strabo Geography 14.1.39

The expression πορφύρεοι μώλωπες (*porphureoi mōlōpes*) is used to refer to the traditional "purple stripes" on the clothing of kings, as in χλαῖναν πορφυρέην, "purple cloak" (*Odyssey* 4.115, 155). But in the distich composed by Daphitas, the expression *porphureoi mōlōpes* is an apostrophe directed at the kings themselves and becomes a depreciative epithet.[35] The LSJ cites this particular passage in Strabo and contextualizes it as "satirically of kings."

Furthermore, in a passage in Dionysus of Halicarnassus' *Roman Antiquities*, *mōlōpas* are the bruises on the body of a young man enslaved by debt, who had been beaten for refusing to give sexual favors as payment:

πολλὰς δὲ διὰ τοῦτο μαστίγων λαβὼν πληγὰς ἐξέδραμεν εἰς τὴν ἀγορὰν καὶ στὰς ἐπὶ μετεώρου τινός, ἔνθα πολλοὺς ἔμελλε τῆς ὕβρεως λήψεσθαι μάρτυρας, τήν τ᾽ ἀκολασίαν τοῦ δανειστοῦ διηγήσατο καὶ τῶν μαστίγων τοὺς μώλωπας ὑπέδειξεν.

And because of this [the young man's refusal to give in to sexual advances], he received many lashes with whips. He then ran to the *forum* and standing on some sort of platform, where he was bound to have many witnesses to this violence, he explained the licentiousness of the money lender and exposed the weals caused by the whips.[36]

Dionysus of Halicarnassus Roman Antiquities 16.5.2

---

[35] In the Irish context we also find a "purple cloak" as symbol of aristocratic status; see Whitfield 2016: 173–174. See the purple tunic in "The Wooing of Étaíne" (Osborne and Best 1938:137–196). In addition, "purple cloak" is one of various epithets and stock phrases used by medieval Irish poets (Shercliff 2015:187–203).

[36] Dionysus makes the point that, unlike a similar case (16.4) where a free man had been lashed for refusing a tribune's sexual advances, in this case (16.5) a former free man had become enslaved because of debt. Upon publicly revealing the bruises (*mōlōpas*) caused by the lashing, he gained the support of the Romans, who henceforth freed any Roman from debt bondage. For the connection between lashing, weals, bruises, and the enslaved, see also Athenaeus *Deipnosophistae* 13.43; Plutarch *Quaestiones convivales* 2.1.

The verb *mōlōpizō* itself means "to beat and bruise severely" and in the passive voice it comes to mean "marked with stripes" (i.e. with bruises).[37] The passage in Dionysus of Halicarnassus above shows that physical punishment was especially associated with the treatment of slaves.[38] Indeed, this is a point Page Dubois has made specifically about the passage from Strabo,[39] namely that Daphitas might be transferring a symbol of slavery, perhaps even a slave epithet ("the striped one," i.e. "bruised") onto the kings, or punning on the word purple, which could simultaneously refer to a king's purple cloaks and to slaves' purple bruises or blemishes.

If one accepts this interpretation, then Daphitas is not only blemishing the kings with his poetic distich, he is also appropriating the meaning of the color purple as a symbol of royalty and using it in the context of slavery. In other words, the appropriation may be a form of resistance, as Dubois suggests.[40] Thus, "purple-striped kings" signifies poetic blame and blemish, the very pun intended by Daphitas in his *loidoria* (mockery) against the rulers in Magnesia, so that *porphureoi mōlōpes* is virtually synonymous with *mōmon* in the sense I have been describing. If the satire, moreover, was meant to refer to some known taboo against "blemished kings" (which Strabo does not say), then the severity of the punishment is all the more understandable, and from the point of view of the insulted royal, even justifiable.[41]

---

[37] Cf. the illustrative use of *memōlōpismenon* in Plutarch as "marked" (as though by beatings) in his *De tuenda sanitate* 2.126c: ἡδοναὶ δὲ σωματικαὶ καὶ ἀπολαύσεις ἔνιαι μὲν οὐδ᾽ ὅλως γένεσιν ἐν νόσῳ λαμβάνουσιν, αἱ δὲ λαμβάνουσαι βραχὺ τὸ οἰκεῖον καὶ οὐ καθαρὸν ἀλλὰ συμπεφυρμένον πολλῷ τῷ ἀλλοτρίῳ καὶ μεμωλωπισμένον ὥσπερ ἐκ ζάλης καὶ χειμῶνος ἀναφέρουσιν. οὐ γὰρ "ἐν πλησμοναῖς Κύπρις," ἀλλὰ μᾶλλον ἐν εὐδίᾳ σαρκὸς καὶ γαλήνῃ καὶ Κύπρις εἰς ἡδονὴν τελευτᾷ, "the pleasures of the body and certain enjoyments do not at all begin in disease, and the ones that do, are short-lived in their own and are not clean, but contaminated with much that is foreign, and blemished, as though by storm and winter. 'It is not in satiety that the Cyprian [Venus] lives,' but rather Venus accomplishes its end in the health of the flesh, and in tranquility."

[38] See Wiedemmann 1981:167–187.

[39] Dubois 2010:116–117.

[40] The adjective *porphureos* ("of purple color") is sometimes used of human complexion: "bright red," "rosy," or "flushing" (Anacreon fr. 2.3 Diehl [Bowra 1961:283] Simonides fr.40 Diehl [Bowra 1961:364], Phrynichus fr. 13 Nauck 1889:723.) The adjective also describes cloth (*Iliad* 8.221, 24.796; *Odyssey*. 4.115), the "surging," or "heaving" of the sea (*Iliad* 1.482, 16.391, 21.326; *Odyssey* 2.428, 11.243), the "gushing" of blood (*Iliad* 17.361), and death (*Iliad* 5.83, 16.334, 20.477). Looking at the Irish context, we find purple blister rising on the forehead of the wicked and foul-mouth man, Bricriú (Stokes 1910: 21, 33).

[41] Fontenrose (1960:83–99) points out that in Valerius Maximus 1.8, in Hesychius of Miletus (*Onomasticon* 14 [4.160 M]) and in *Suda* 99 the version of the story of Daphitas' insult against the king and the ensuing punishment is different from Strabo's version of crucifixion (83). In this other version, "Daphidas" (Fontenrose's spelling), who was a consummate satirist, attempted to trick even the Pythia with a deceptive question, and for this Attalus had him thrown off a cliff (83). Fontenrose points out that crucifixion, as well as throwing one off a cliff, was a punishment mostly reserved for the "lowborn" and slaves (97–98). In Fontenrose's view Daphitas was a sophist espousing doctrines favorable to a rebel and slave uprising, and his insults were

Nevertheless, with Strabo's passage we have a Greek illustration of the relationship between poet and king shaped by blame, not praise, with direct reference to blemishes, expressed as a pun. From this, I advance the interpretation that *mōmon anapsai* is the Homeric illustration of such a relationship.[42] Therefore, Homeric *mōmon anapsai*, Strabo's *porphureoi mōlōpes*, and the Irish *áer* operate along the same sociocultural bandwidth.[43]

4.3 *Mōmos* and *Mōmeuō*: Begrudging and Gluttony

One of the most prominent vices of the suitors is gluttony. In order to make a connection between gluttony, blame, and reproach, I will now consider one specialized meaning of the verb *mōmeuō*, that is, "to begrudge," in the specific context of sacrificial feasting and the apportioning of food. I refer to a passage in Hesiod's *Works and Days* where the poet warns those attending a sacrifice not "to begrudge" or "criticize" (*mōmeuein*) the "consuming" fire which takes away the god's portion:

... μηδ' ἱεροῖσιν ἐπ' αἰθομένοισι κυρήσας
<u>μωμεύειν</u> ἀίδηλα· θεός νύ τι καὶ τὰ νεμεσσᾷ.

---

specifically aimed at Attalus III, a harsh and thin-skinned ruler, not at the other Attalid royals as some have proposed (86).

[42] Incidentally, in the Thersites episode we also find "blemishes," or rather the "bloody welt" rising on Thersites' back after Odysseus beats him: the words there are *smōdix ... haimatoessa* (*Iliad* 2.267), a near synonym to *mōlōpes porphureoi*.

[43] In addition, the word *ail* (invective) in *Siege of Howth* (Book of Leinster) offers an example of the overlap between invective and blemish. Athirne, a poet from Ulster, was known for his "ruthless exactions":
"This is the way Atherne [sic] went thereafter, to Leinster... And they [the men of Leinster] came ... to meet him and to offer jewels and treasures, not to come into the country, so that he might not leave invectives [*ailche*, accusative plural of *ail*] ... Now this is what he bore in his mind, great invectives [*ailche*] to leave on the Leinster-men [sic]... So then he made a demand of the men of the south of Leinster in Brestine, (and he said) he saw not of jewels or treasures aught [what the Leinster men had offered] that he would take from them, but he would leave an *ail bréthre* (verbal insult) on them forever, so that they should not hold up their faces before the Gael, unless they gave him the jewel that was best on the hill" (Stokes 1887:51). Watkins (1962:114-118) comments on the Irish word *-antar* (117) ['is blemished'] occurring in a verse from the old law tract concerning the rights and responsibilities of poets (Gwynn 1942:13-60). The context for the verses, which Watkins quotes is the capacity of praise to cleanse blemish formulated as a metaphor of polished silver: *do-aisic a dath / dia aír -antar / aiged cach airgit / acht co ngúairiu -glantar*). Watkins suggests a reading of these verses which interprets the meaning of *-antar* as the passive voice of **anaid* ('blemishes,' 3rd person singular present), not its homophone *anaid* (he/she/it 'remains'). Hence, he translates these verses thus: "[it] [sic] recovers its colour if it *be blemished* by satire / the face of every silver provided it be polished with a bristle." Interestingly, Watkins observes that *anaid* "represents an old athematic laryngeal (*set*) base cognate with Gk ὄνομαι 'blame,' likewise athematic in the Homeric form ὤνατο."

Do not, while attending burning sacrifice,
begrudge the consumed portion, the god disapproves of this also.

Hesiod *Works and Days* 755–756

While some translations of this passage have rendered *mōmeuein aidēla* as "criticize," or "mock the mysteries," I follow Robertson's interpretation,[44] for whom the meaning of *aidēla* as "mysteries" (derived from "invisible" or "make invisible," *a-idēlos*) is improbable. The immediate context (a list of injunctions against taboos regulating common behaviors), and its occurrences in Hesiod and Homer, where it appears as the common epithet for fire, *pur aidēlon* (e.g. *Iliad* 2.455) seems to support the meaning "destructive," rather than "invisible."[45] Robertson's argument rests on philological considerations of the word *aidēla*, which he concludes is best understood as "consuming" or "destructive," rather than "unseen," based on the fact that "to make invisible or unseen" is often figurative for "make disappear" as the verb *aistoō* ("disappear", "annihilate") indicates: ὡς ἔμ' ἀϊστώσειαν Ὀλύμπια δώματ' ἔχοντες, / ἠέ μ' ἐϋπλόκαμος βάλοι Ἄρτεμις, "I wish those who have their homes on Olympus would make me disappear / or Artemis would destroy me" (*Odyssey* 20.79-80).[46] Robertson concludes by interpreting *aidēla* as the object of *mōmeuein* and translates it as the "consumed" offering. He does not explain the shift from the active "consuming" (i.e. fire) to the passive "consumed" (offering), but if *aidēla* represents "consuming fire," as he proposes (rightly, I think, rejecting the adverbial meaning "secretly"), then the injunction would be for the attendee at a sacrifice to avoid begrudging that which is "ablaze," in the process of being consumed by the fire.

Leaving other nuanced interpretations of *aidēla* aside for the moment, I agree with Robertson and take the verb *mōmeuein* in this context as "begrudging" or "enviously resenting," rather than "criticizing" overtly: "*mōmeuein* as usual expresses the envy of a deprived onlooker."[47] Thus, if *mōmeuein* allows for

---

44   Robertson 1969:164–169.
45   Other instances of such a meaning include Hesiod frr. 60.2, 67a.5 (Merkelbach-West); *Iliad* 2.455, 5.880, 5.897, 9.436, 11.155, 21.220. Cf. Empedocles (fr. 109 Diels): γαίῃ μὲν γὰρ γαῖαν ὀπώπαμεν, ὕδατι δ' ὕδωρ, / αἰθέρι δ' αἰθέρα δῖαν, ἀτὰρ πυρὶ πῦρ ἀΐδηλον, / στοργῇ δὲ στοργήν, νεῖκος δέ τε νείκεϊ λυγρῷ "we perceive water through water, air through bright air, consuming/destructive fire through fire."
46   See also *aphanizō*: οἱ δὲ οὐ πολλῷ ὕστερον ἠφάνισάν τε αὐτοὺς καὶ οὐδεὶς ᾔσθετο ὅτῳ τρόπῳ ἕκαστος διεφθάρη, "They [Spartans], however, not long afterward made them [the Helots] disappear [i.e. murdered them], and no one ever knew in what way each of them perished (Thucydides 4.80); cf. *Odyssey* 10.258–260 for the literal meaning of "disappearing," yet with the clear sense of disaster: αὐτὰρ ἐγὼν ὑπέμεινα, ὀϊσάμενος δόλον εἶναι. / οἱ δ' ἅμ' ἀϊστώθησαν ἀολλέες, οὐδέ τις αὐτῶν / ἐξεφάνη, "but I stayed, thinking this was a trick / but all of them disappeared, none of them / appeared."
47   Robertson 1969: 169.

the meaning "to envy," then *mōmos* and *phthonos*, are linked, perhaps in ways similar to their representation in Callimachus' *Hymn to Apollo* (113). In the hymn Callimachus has Apollo formulate the poet's (Callimachus) own programmatic argument, that slender poetry is cleaner, purer than the lengthy kind (i.e. epic). Callimachus then hails the god's words by condemning *Mōmos* (Criticism) and *Phthonos* (Envy) personified : χαῖρε ἄναξ: ὁ δὲ Μῶμος, ἵν' ὁ Φθόνος, ἔνθα νέοιτο, "Hail lord: but *Mōmos*, he should dwell there (perish) where *Phthonos* dwells." Although the context in which Callimachus present *Mōmos* and *Phthonos* (the very program of Hellenistic poetry) is far removed from the epic, the linking of *mōmos* with *phthonos* is applicable to the suitors in their relentless intent to criticize Telemachus and destroy Odysseus' wealth, out of their envy of Odysseus' position as king and Penelope's husband. In view of Robertson's interpretation of *mōmeuein* as "begrudging," the *mōmos-phthonos* connection spelled out in Callimachus as a matter of poetic style, in the *Odyssey* it becomes an ethical matter with social implications for kingship.

But to return to *aidēla*: the suitors are a "consuming" and "destructive" force, much like fire.[48] Accordingly, their characterization as "devourers" (*edontes*)[49] is articulated in the epithet *aidēlon* used to describe them as a group: ἀνδρῶν μνηστήρων ἐσορᾶν ἀΐδηλον ὅμιλον, "to look at the destructive gathering of the suitors" (*Odyssey* 16.29).[50] Furthermore, coveting meat and begrudging (*mōmeuein*) another's portion, even the gods' share, recalls the literal meaning of *bōmolokhia*, as we have already seen, that is, "attack" or "ambush at the altar" for getting meat.[51] Naturally, anyone attending a sacrifice would have occasion to begrudge (*mōmeuein*) any portion of meat left to burn at the altar.[52]

As *mōmon anapsai* can be a periphrasis for *mōmeuein*, then "begrudging" is another way to translate and interpret Antinous' words. The suitor could be warning Telemachus "not to begrudge" the meat they apportion to themselves from the hero's large stock. Such a response would be entirely appropriate, because in Telemachus' speech at the assembly, the weightiest charge against the suitors is their consumption of meat (*Odyssey* 2.49, 56–58). Indeed, their

---

48 Ares himself is described as *aidēlos* (*Odyssey* 8.309).
49 The description of the suitors as "devouring," or "devourers" (*edontes*) of Odysseus' livelihood is repeated many times: *Odyssey* 1.160, 1.248, 1.250–251, 2.204, 11.116, 14.17, 14.81, 14.377, 15.12–13, 17.331–332, 21.69, and at several other verses.
50 Compare with *pur aidēlon* (*Iliad* 2.455, 9.436, 11.155).
51 See also Isenberg 1975:271–273 on sacrificial meat.
52 The part reserved for the gods was typically the thigh bone wrapped in fat, with small cuts from every limb placed on it (Oxford Classical Dictionary 1996:1344), so that the best parts were for people's consumption, which would make the begrudging of the meager part reserved for the god even more improper and insolent.

gluttony is a signifier of blemish itself, and it is especially graphic and grotesque as the narrative approaches their doom:

> ... μνηστῆρσι δὲ Παλλὰς Ἀθήνη
> ἄσβεστον γέλω ὦρσε, παρέπλαγξεν δὲ νόημα.
> οἱ δ᾽ ἤδη γναθμοῖσι γελώων ἀλλοτρίοισιν,
> αἱμοφόρυκτα δὲ δὴ κρέα ἤσθιον· ὄσσε δ᾽ ἄρα σφέων
> δακρυόφιν πίμπλαντο, γόον δ᾽ ὠΐετο θυμός.

> ... and among the suitors Pallas Athena
> raised unquenchable laughter, and confused their minds
> and now they were laughing with strange jaws
> the meat they were eating was smeared with blood, and their eyes
> were filling with tears, and their spirit seemed to anticipate their
> wailing.

> *Odyssey* 20. 345-349[53]

Moreover, we already know that the suitors are guests who bring nothing to the common table: no food, no praise, and no stories.[54] Even a beggar or a slave contributes his share by working. Consider Telemachus' words about Odysseus as beggar: οὐ γὰρ ἀεργὸν ἀνέξομαι ὅς κεν ἐμῆς γε / χοίνικος ἅπτηται,[55] καὶ τηλόθεν εἰληλουθώς, "I will not allow anyone to be idle, / whoever touches my portion of meal, even if he comes from afar," *Odyssey* 19.27-28). In fact, the suitors are gluttonous and *aergoi* ("idle," "lazy"). They continuously covet and waste the palace's wealth, plan to usurp Telemachus' rightful inheritance, and resent Penelope's delay and rejection of them.

4.4 *Pharmakos*: Scapegoats and Sacrifice

As in Irish satire, blemishing someone with words can be a political and social phenomenon akin to ostracism, which may lead to physical punishment of the victim. In Greek tradition this phenomenon is expressed in ritualized form, that is, the sacrifice itself of a scapegoat called a *pharmakos*, or it is the person chosen

---

[53] Compare the fact that Penelope calls Antinous a *margos*, a word that stands for "gluttonous" and "mad" (*Odyssey* 16.421).

[54] By contrast Odysseus is himself the perfect guest. Though destitute in Alcinous' court, he delights the Phaeacians with his own Odyssey (books 9-12). In fact, the idea that Odysseus controls his version of the *Odyssey* recalls Danek 1998, where the author argues that the *Odyssey* indirectly admits alternative versions of the *Odyssey* contextually and thematically.

[55] I have mentioned this example above in connection to the meaning of *haptomai* as the "touching," or "taking of" food.

to stand for the ills besetting a given community, such as famine (*Hipponax* fr. 128 W) or wrongdoing (Hipponax fr. 115 W). [56] There are also cases involving kings as scapegoats, even if they are not strictly considered *pharmakoi*.[57] So-called famine-demons (scapegoats) can be expelled, beaten, or stoned.[58] With this social context in mind, it is reasonable to consider the suitors in relation to the *pharmakos* ritual tradition, especially the aspect of the ritual whereby the victim is loaded down with food and beaten.[59] For instance, in book 20 a slave woman in Odysseus' palace says she has been overworked by the suitors' demands and prays that this dinner she is now preparing will become their last meal:[60]

Ζεῦ πάτερ, ὅς τε θεοῖσι καὶ ἀνθρώποισιν ἀνάσσεις,
ἦ μεγάλ᾽ ἐβρόντησας ἀπ᾽ οὐρανοῦ ἀστερόεντος,
οὐδέ ποθι νέφος ἐστί· τέρας νύ τεῳ τόδε φαίνεις.
κρῆνον νῦν καὶ ἐμοὶ δειλῇ <u>ἔπος</u>, ὅττι κεν εἴπω·
μνηστῆρες πύματόν τε καὶ ὕστατον ἤματι τῷδε
ἐν μεγάροις Ὀδυσῆος ἑλοίατο δαῖτ᾽ ἐρατεινήν,
οἳ δή μοι καμάτῳ θυμαλγέϊ γούνατ᾽ ἔλυσαν
ἄλφιτα τευχούσῃ· νῦν ὕστατα δειπνήσειαν.

---

[56] Compare scholia on Aristophanes *Knights* 1136c: "exceedingly low born" (*lian agenneis*) in Koster 1969 *ad loc.* In Aristophanes, *pharmakos* designates "low born" (*Frogs* 733). in Strabo, "criminals," "guilty," as well as the "exceedingly ugly" (*Geography* 10.2.9); and in Tzetzes, "deformed" (*Chiliades* 5.731). Compare Pliny *Natural History* 36.5. This is the account of Hipponax's extreme facial ugliness, which the sculptor Bupalus decided to represent in stone for public amusement. Hipponax's iambic attacks were so vicious that Bupalus hanged himself. The potential violence that follows from the iambs is also associated with Archilochus' insults of Lycambes' daughters. (fr. 30 W). The word *pharmakós* (masculine) here, with accent on the ultima, is to be distinguished from *phármakon* (neuter), "medicinal plant," "remedy," with accent on the antepenult (*Odyssey* 10.317, 327). See Compton 2006:3–18 for instructive details and analysis of the evidence of the φαρμακός ritual.

[57] For example, the legend of king Codrus in Plato *Symposium* (208d) has it that he dressed as a beggar before arranging for his own death, a motif that brings up common themes related to the *pharmakos*. Of course we think of Odysseus, the *basileus*, dressed as beggar. In other words, for the noble to undergo experiences normally afflicting the ignoble, they must disguise themselves sometimes through cross-dressing, even metamorphosis, and thus become another. For other such themes, see Compton 2006; compare Steiner 2009. The punishment against scapegoats included expulsion and death (Hipponax frr. 104 W; 5–10 W)

[58] Compton 2006:3–18.

[59] Faraone 2004; compare Compton 2006.

[60] Following Faraone (2004), the *pharmakos* ritual is an incantation and expulsion curse recited in verse. Faraone further makes the point that, although the traditional interpretation of Hipponax fr. 128 W is that the poem is a parody of epic diction with hexameter verses and epic echoes ("Tell me Muse"), this does not exclude its ritualized and recitative aspect. Another epic echo in this passage is the frequent Homeric formula "by the shores of the barren [or loud-roaring] sea," παρὰ θῖν᾽ ἁλὸς ἀτρυγέτοιο (*Iliad* 1.34 1.316; *Odyssey* 1.72).

Father Zeus, who rules over gods and men,
how loudly have you thundered from the starry heaven,
but there is no cloud there. You are surely revealing this omen to
    someone.
Fulfill now also for me, being wretched this _epos_ [= Irish _ferb_ (from
    Latin _verbum_)] which I recite:
may the suitors on this day and for the last time
hold their beloved feast in Odysseus' halls.
These men who have loosened my knees with sorrowful labor
While I made them meals, may they now feast for the last time.

Odyssey 20.112–119

An especially interesting representation of the *pharmakos* tradition in connection to food and gluttony is again expressed in Hipponax (fr. 128 W). The poet attacks his enemy precisely for behaving badly.

Μοῦσα μοι Εὐρυμεδοντιάδεα τὴν ροντοχάρυβδιν,
τὴν ἐν γαστρὶ μάχαιραν, ὅς ἐσθίει οὐ κατὰ κόσμον,
ἐννεφ', ὅπως ψηφῖδι ⟨ ⟩ κακὸν οἶτον ολεῖται
βουλῆ δημοσίη παρὰ θῖν' ἁλὸς ἀτρυγέτοιο.

Tell me Muse of the Offspring of the One-Who-Rules-Widely, the Sea-Swallower, the Knife-in the-belly, who eats without limit-in order
    that
<wretch> may lose his wretched life by stoning (chased) down to the shore of the fruitless sea, according to the wish of the people.[61]

Hipponax fr. 128 W

Insofar as the suitors are themselves the ills besetting Ithaca, they fit the ritual pattern of royal scapegoats. In fact, all who stand for righteousness in the *Odyssey*, particularly the swineherd Eumaeus and the trusted old maid, Eurycleia,

---

[61] Translation by Faraone 2004:210. Faraone includes an apparatus criticus to this fragment to indicate the various readings (1 Εὐρυμεδοντιάδεω Wilamowitz 2 ἐγγαστριμάχαιραν libri praeter E; ἐν γαστρὶ μάχαιραν West 3 ⟨κακὸς⟩ Cobet; ⟨κακῇ⟩ Musurus; ⟨κρυφεῖς⟩ West ὅληται codd.; ὀλεῖται Cobet). West's translation interprets the word ψηφῖδι, not as 'stone, hence stoning', but as 'vote': "Tell me, O Muse, of Eurymedontiades the / Charybdis, / him of the gastric carvers, who eats in irregular / fashion: / tell how amid the shingle the wretch will wretchedly perish / by the *vote* of the people beside the limitless seashore (1993:123)" I have chosen to quote Faraone's translation, but a reading that takes the voting 'pebble,' or 'stone' as a play on words for casting (voting) someone out (the scapegoat) violently (by stoning) may be possible.

agree that the suitors are a scourge, who will eventually consume Telemachus' possessions if they are not prevented from doing so. Like "famine-demons," the suitors stand for pollution in Odysseus' house, which the hero must expunge. Thus, *mnēstērophonia* itself, Odysseus' *mega ergon*, though vicious, becomes partly acculturated and partly naturalized by the use of a simile comparing the hero to a "lion mauling its victim" (*Odyssey* 22.402–403).[62] Indeed, at the sight of the murdered young men, the loyal servant Eurycleia begins to perform a ritualized cry (*ololugē*)[63] in praise of the hero's bloodthirsty slaughter, described by her as a "venerable deed":

ἡ δ᾽ ὡς οὖν νέκυάς τε καὶ ἄσπετον ἔσιδεν αἷμα,
ἴθυσέν ῥ᾽ <u>ὀλολύξαι</u>, ἐπεὶ <u>μέγα</u> ἔσιδεν <u>ἔργον</u>·
ἀλλ᾽ Ὀδυσεὺς κατέρυκε καὶ ἔσχεθεν ἱεμένην περ.

And when she saw the bodies and the unspeakable slaughter
she started to <u>raise a cry of prayer</u>, seeing the <u>great deed</u>.
But Odysseus prevented and held her back, though she was jubilant.

Odyssey 22.407–409

Thus, *mnēstērophonia* can stand for the *pharmakos* ritual. In this respect Telemachus did succeed in *blemishing* the suitors (with words) at the assembly in book 1, while Odysseus transformed them into scapegoats in book 24.[64] The large band of suitors become yet another monster for Odysseus to vanquish, and scapegoats to be expunged. The analogy with scapegoats becomes relevant because while sacrificial animals must be "whole" (*teleios*),[65] "unblemished" (*amōmos*), the suitors are to be sacrificed precisely because they are "unwholesome," "incomplete" (*ateleis*), and monstrous. The term *teleios* (*Iliad* 1.66 24.34) is used not only for an unblemished, hence perfect animal, but also for a "married man," because marriage makes masculinity whole.[66] Odysseus

---

[62] At *Iliad* 3.197, Odysseus is compared to a ram moving through a great flock of white ewes (ἀρνειῷ μιν ἔγωγε ἐΐσκω πηγεσιμάλλῳ / ὅς τ᾽ οἰῶν μέγα πῶϋ διέρχεται ἀργεννάων) to signify his leading status, in contrast to Achilles, who is compared to a lion (*Iliad* 20.165, 24.41).

[63] This sacred cry is used in animal sacrifice also at *Odyssey* 3.450; compare with a prayer accompanied by grain offering (*Odyssey* 4.767).

[64] In sacrificial rituals the animal to be sacrificed was consecrated, crowned, sprinkled with grains, or otherwise decorated before being led for slaughter.

[65] For kings, compare *Odyssey* 19.109: *basilēos amumonos*, "of a blemish-free king."

[66] See Steinrück 2008:31–32. His discussion on the importance of being married illustrates the generational tension between older and younger men around marital status.

sacrifices them, thereby cleansing the palace of the pollution they represent, and finally fulfilling Telemachus' words from book 1:

> ἐγὼ δὲ θεοὺς ἐπιβώσομαι αἰὲν ἐόντας,
> αἴ κέ ποθι Ζεὺς δῷσι παλίντιτα ἔργα γενέσθαι·
> ἤποινοί κεν ἔπειτα δόμων ἔντοσθεν ὄλοισθε. [67]

> and so I call upon the gods who are forever
> if ever Zeus should grant these deeds to come to pass
> without atonement then, may you perish inside the halls.

Odyssey 1.379-380

4.5 *Mōmos* and *Aitia*: Origin of Trouble

Antinous attempts to shift responsibility (*aitia*) for the troubles in the palace from the suitors to Penelope: σοὶ δ' οὔ τι μνηστῆρες Ἀχαιῶν <u>αἴτιοί</u> εἰσιν, "For your information, in no way are the suitors <u>guilty/responsible</u> among the Achaeans" (*Odyssey* 2.87). Antinous defends the suitors' behavior as rightful indignation at Penelope's deceit, her cleverness (*dolos*),[68] which is ironically a highly valued talent, indeed a distinguishing mark. For the suitors, Penelope is both good and bad; she is the embodiment of praise and blame:

> πάντας μέν ἔλπει, καὶ ὑπίσχεται ἀνδρὶ ἑκάστῳ
> ἀγγελίας προϊεῖσα. νόος δέ οἱ ἄλλα μενοινᾷ.
> ἡ δὲ δόλον τόνδ' ἄλλον ἐνὶ φρεσὶ μερμήριξε·
> στησαμένη μέγαν ἱστὸν ἐνὶ μεγάροισιν ὕφαινε,
> λεπτὸν καὶ περίμετρον

> She gives hope to all, and holds out promise to each man,
> sending out messages, but in her mind, she plans otherwise,
> and this other trick she has contrived in her spirit:
> standing at the large loom in the *megaron* she wove
> an elegant and wide shroud.

Odyssey 2.91–95

---

[67] Telemachus' wish that the suitors would "perish" (ὄλοισθε) parallels Hipponax's fragment 128 W, which expresses the same curse.

[68] For example, at *Odyssey* 9.282 Odysseus' clever words (*doliois epeessi*) lead to the ambush of Polyphemus. Compare also *dolophroneōn* ("cunning mind") as an epithet for Odysseus (*Odyssey* 18.51).

Previously, I discussed the word *aitios* in its juridical sense compared to *mōmos*, particularly in Zeus' speech (*Odyssey* 1.32), where *aitios* is used with an emphatically negative connotation, not just as the "cause," but as the "cause of trouble." The suitors protest that they are not the *aitioi* (the cause) of troubles in Penelope's palace, but at the start of the slaughter of the suitors (*mnēstērophonia*) following Antinous' death, Eurymachus cowardly blames Antinous in order to spare his own life. In this blame game Eurymachus' words make clear that competition for the kingship was and had always been the central motive for the suitors' behavior:[69]

ἀλλ' ὁ μὲν ἤδη κεῖται ὃς αἴτιος ἔπλετο πάντων,
Ἀντίνοος· οὗτος γὰρ ἐπίηλεν τάδε ἔργα,
οὔ τι γάμου τόσσον κεχρημένος οὐδὲ χατίζων,
ἀλλ' φρονέων, τά οἱ οὐκ ἐτέλεσσε Κρονίων,
ὄφρ' Ἰθάκης κατὰ δῆμον ἐϋκτιμένης βασιλεύοι
αὐτός, ἀτὰρ σὸν παῖδα κατακτείνειε λοχήσας.

But now he [Antinous] lies dead, the aitios, who carried it all out,
Antinous. For he [Antinous] it was who brought about these deeds,
not so much for need or desire for marriage,
but considering other things, which for him the son the Cronus did
    not fulfill,
in order that in the well-ordered land of Ithaca, he would rule as king
while lying in ambush to kill your son
himself.

Odyssey 22.48–53

4.6 *Mōmeuein* and *Nemesis*: The Talk of the People

When Telemachus worries that he may incur the reproach of the people if he sends Penelope back to her father, as Antinous suggests (*Odyssey* 2.113–114), he uses the word *nemesis*[70] (*Odyssey* 2.136.). Penelope too uses *nemesis* when in her response to the pressure the suitors continue to exert to force her to finally choose a husband from among them. Antinous expands on the reasons why the suitors continue to linger in the palace halls for so long. He mentions Penelope's

---

[69] *Aitia* as a "wrong" is one of the definitions of *pharmakos* given in Strabo, as I mentioned above.
[70] *Nemesis* also occurs as "blame of the people" or "public shame" (*Odyssey* 6.286) and fear of god (*Odyssey* 22.39–40). Compare *elenkhea* for "public talk" (*Odyssey* 21.329); *dēmou phēmis*, "the talk of the people" (*Odyssey* 14.239).

excuses for delaying the marriage, her weaving. At first Penelope's concerns over the *nemesis* from other women sounded legitimate:

κοῦροι, ἐμοὶ μνηστῆρες, ἐπεὶ θάνε δῖος Ὀδυσσεύς,
μίμνετ᾽ ἐπειγόμενοι τὸν ἐμὸν γάμονεἰς ὅ κε φᾶρος
ἐκτελέσω, μή μοι μεταμώνια νήματ᾽ ὄληται,
Λαέρτῃ ἥρωϊ ταφήϊον, εἰς ὅτε κέν μιν
μοῖρ᾽ ὀλοὴ καθέλῃσι τανηλεγέος θανάτοιο,
μή τίς μοι κατὰ δῆμον Ἀχαιϊάδων <u>νεμεσήσῃ</u>,

Young men, my suitors, since noble Odysseus has died,
have patience, while desiring my marriage, and wait until
I have finished this robe—lest my spinning is given to the winds,
    destroyed.
It is a shroud for the hero Laertes, for that time when
cruel fate of merciless death takes him down.
lest some Achaean women among the people should <u>reproach</u> me.

Odyssey 2.96–101

Penelope's expressed anxieties over public reproach parallels Nausicaa's worries about being seen with Odysseus. Nausicaa, the young daughter of King Alcinous of the Phaeacians, tells Odysseus that it would not be proper for her to enter town accompanied by a stranger. She explains that people might "blame" her. In her speech, we find both *nemesis* and the verbal form *mōmeuein*:

τῶν ἀλεείνω <u>φῆμιν ἀδευκέα</u>, μή τις ὀπίσσω
<u>μωμεύῃ</u>· μάλα δ᾽ εἰσὶν <u>ὑπερφίαλοι</u> κατὰ δῆμον·
καί νύ τις ὧδ᾽ εἴπῃσι κακώτερος ἀντιβολήσας·
"τίς δ᾽ ὅδε Ναυσικάᾳ ἕπεται καλός τε μέγας τε
277ξεῖνος; ποῦ δέ μιν εὗρε; πόσις νύ οἱ ἔσσεται αὐτῇ
. . . .
283. . . ἦ γὰρ τούσδε γ᾽ ἀτιμάζει κατὰ δῆμον
Φαίηκας, τοί μιν μνῶνται πολέες τε καὶ ἐσθλοί."
ὣς ἐρέουσιν, ἐμοὶ δέ κ᾽ <u>ὀνείδεα</u> ταῦτα γένοιτο.
καὶ δ᾽ ἄλλῃ <u>νεμεσῶ</u>, ἥ τις τοιαῦτά γε ῥέζοι,
ἥ τ᾽ ἀέκητι φίλων πατρὸς καὶ μητρὸς ἐόντων
ἀνδράσι μίσγηται πρίν γ᾽ ἀμφάδιον γάμον ἐλθεῖν.

I want to avoid the <u>wicked words</u> of those men, lest from now on
    someone
might <u>blame me</u>; for there are indeed many <u>insolent</u> men among the
    people.

Now some of the lowest types might argue thus:
"Who is this man that follows Nausicaa, handsome and tall—
a foreigner? Where did she find him? He might become her husband ...
She really insults the people—for among the Phaeacians here, to be
    sure,
there are suitors, many and noble."
This is how they will talk, and these words would be a <u>reproach</u>
    against me.
But I, too, would <u>blame</u> [hold <u>nemesis</u>] the woman who might do
    such things,
who, against mother and father still living,
would have sex with men before coming into legitimate marriage.

Odyssey 6.273–277; 283–288

Nausicaa indicates that the people would "reproach" her (μωμεύῃ, 274) from
then on (ὀπίσσω, 273) suggesting that blame can become permanent. In other
words, Nausicaa understands that the *vox populi* can become an "infamous
song," or "wicked speech" (φῆμιν ἀδευκέα, 273),[71] censorious and hostile. She is
aware of those who might be especially wicked (τις ... κακώτερος, 275), inclined
to argue (ἀντιβολήσας, 275) like a *philopsogos* or *philomōmos*.[72] From Nausicaa's
considerations we can clearly infer that one social function of blame speech is
the maintenance of social norms, in this case the regulation of women's behavior.
Thus, the verb *nemesaō* (nemesis)—"to feel just resentment," and "to be indignant"—asserts the community's values by blaming the socially unacceptable.[73]

Notwithstanding the suitors' wicked speech,[74] Nausicaa herself, steeped in
these same values, later admits that she too would "blame" or "resent" (νεμεσῶ,
286) another woman if she were to "have sex"   (μίσγηται, 288) with men before

---

[71] Compare *Odyssey* 21.255.

[72] The distinction between *philopsogos* and *philomōmos* is that *philopsogos* indicates a temporary
state, while *philomōmos* may refer to an essential quality, as we see in this passage in Plato's
Protagoras 346c1-6: ὦ Πιττακέ, οὐ διὰ ταῦτά σε <u>ψέγω</u>, ὅτι εἰμὶ <u>φιλόψογος</u>, / . . . οὐ γάρ εἰμι
<u>φιλόμωμος</u>, "Oh Pittacus, I do not blame you for these things because I am <u>inclined to blame</u>,
for I am not a *philomōmos*." Plato here is paraphrasing Simonides' verses, which are themselves a
meditation on the desirability of restraining from blame speech: ἔμοιγ' ἐξαρκεῖ / ὃς ἂν μὴ κακὸς
ᾖ μηδ' ἄγαν ἀπάλαμνος, / εἰδώς τ' ὀνησίπολιν δίκαν / ὑγιὴς ἀνήρ· οὔ μιν ἐγὼ / <u>μωμήσομαι</u>— /
τῶν γὰρ ἠλιθίων ἀπείρων γενέθλα, / . . . πάντα τοι καλά, τοῖσί τ' αἰσχρὰ μὴ μέμεικται, "To me it
suffices / if one is not evil, nor excessively reckless, / if he knows how to be beneficial to order. /
Such a man is sound, / thus, I will not <u>blame</u> him— / for the generations of fools is endless, / . . .
all best things are among those that are not mixed with shamelessness." Cf. also Pindar 181 S-M:
ὁ γὰρ ἐξ οἴκου ποτὶ <u>μῶμον ἔπαινος</u> κίρναται, "for it is especially from one's own home [commu-
nity], that praise (*epainos*) is mixed with <u>blame</u> (*mōmos*)."

[73] The satirical poet's criticisms against kings are often identical with the people's criticism, so
that the poet is the mouthpiece of the people: see Dumézil 1943:230–234.

[74] Compare *kakagorian* (Pindar *Pythian* 2.53).

marriage.[75] Just as Penelope worries about the "justified" blame that other women might cast against her (*Odyssey* 2.101–102), so too does Nausicaa understand why and how others might blame her, even as she calls them "insolent" (*huperphialoi*, 274). Therefore, she recognizes that blame is a complicated matter: it is both individual criticism and social stigma. In our passage, the Phaeacian men reproach Nausicaa for choosing to "go with" an outsider, a "foreigner." Accordingly, Odysseus as the outsider will soon be challenged and even taunted by some of the Phaeacian suitors, foreshadowing what Odysseus will encounter at home in Ithaca.

The verb *mōmeuein* in Nausicaa's speech above fundamentally expresses the men's resentment, even envy (*phthonos*) of Odysseus. The hero (and stranger) poses a threat not only for his transgression of social norms (seen with a local girl), but also from the sexual tension inherent in Odysseus' appeal as foreign male: "Could he be a shipwreck survivor, or maybe even a god?" (*Odyssey* 6.278–281). Moreover, Nausicaa says that the envious suitors might say that the foreigner is "tall" and "handsome." In verses 273–279, Nausicaa is actually speaking in the character of an ordinary man: that is, she acts out one of them, and in his persona she can say what would be inappropriate for her to say. In this way, she is able to send Odysseus a double message: he needs to know how to enter the town without compromising her reputation, and she lets him know that his appeal is a legitimate threat to the local men, because she is the one who finds him "tall" and "handsome" and would have him as her husband (*Odyssey* 6.242–243): πρόσθεν μὲν γὰρ δή μοι ἀεικέλιος δέατ' εἶναι, / νῦν δὲ θεοῖσιν ἔοικε, "[this man] who before seemed to be unattractive / but now he seems like the gods").[76] Therefore, Odysseus is a contender, and the athletic contest to which the Phaeacian young men challenge him conforms to the traditional narrative and rhetoric associated with suitors and *agōn*, that is, the bride-winning contest (*Odyssey* 8.133–137).

---

[75] It is noteworthy, however, that in 283 the people's "evil speech" is not directly about women having sex with men, but specifically about choosing a man outside the group, that is, "a foreigner" (*xeinos*). Compare *Odyssey* 23.218–219: οὐδέ κεν Ἀργείη Ἑλένη, Διὸς ἐκγεγαυῖα, / <u>ἀνδρὶ</u> <u>παρ' ἀλλοδαπῷ</u> ἐμίγη φιλότητι καὶ εὐνῇ, "nor would Argive Helen, the offspring of Zeus / join in love with a <u>man from another land</u>."

[76] Following their initial encounter, Odysseus bathed, and Athena helped him to look attractive. Nausicaa's words are reminiscent of Sappho 31.1–2: φαίνεταί μοι κῆνος ἴσος θέοισιν / ἔμμεν' ὤνηρ, "That man seems to me [beautiful] like the gods." I am aware of the various interpretive possibilities of this verse (see Furley 2000, for example); however, my point is simply to underscore the sexual attraction that Nausicaa feels towards Odysseus. Nausicaa's speech offers an interesting parallel to Antinous' speech. Like Nausicaa, Antinous performs Penelope, speaking in her voice; he highlights her duplicitousness through mimicry, while downplaying the suitors' faults. Likewise, Antinous articulates the suitors' ambiguous feelings towards Penelope—they like both her virtuousness and cleverness.

4.7 *Polu Prōton, Polutropos*: Ruler in Contest and Speech

Odysseus at first does not want to compete (*Odyssey* 8.153–154), but he is taunted by Euryalus (Odyssey 8.158), one of Nausicaa's suitors (*Odyssey* 8.159–164), the one who most closely exemplifies the arrogance that defines Penelope's suitors. Angry at Euryalus' "soul-biting insult"(*thumodakēs ... muthos*, 8.185), Odysseus delivers a response which is especially significant for its didactic quality, namely, an instruction to rulers, or to those aspiring to rulership, on the importance of proper speech (praise, not blame):

> ξεῖν', <u>οὐ καλὸν ἔειπες·</u> ἀτασθάλῳ ἀνδρὶ ἔοικας.
> οὕτως οὐ πάντεσσι θεοὶ χαρίεντα διδοῦσιν
> ἀνδράσιν, οὔτε φυὴν οὔτ' ἄρ φρένας οὔτ' ἀγορητύν.
> ἄλλος μὲν γάρ τ' εἶδος ἀκιδνότερος πέλει ἀνήρ,
> ἀλλὰ θεὸς μορφὴν ἔπεσι στέφει, οἱ δέ τ' ἐς αὐτὸν
> τερπόμενοι λεύσσουσιν· ὁ δ' <u>ἀσφαλέως ἀγορεύει</u>
> <u>αἰδοῖ μειλιχίῃ,</u> μετὰ δὲ πρέπει ἀγρομένοισιν,
> ἐρχόμενον δ' ἀνὰ ἄστυ θεὸν ὣς εἰσορόωσιν.
> ἄλλος δ' αὖ εἶδος μὲν ἀλίγκιος ἀθανάτοισιν,
> ἀλλ' οὔ οἱ χάρις ἀμφιπεριστέφεται ἐπέεσσιν,
> ὡς καὶ σοὶ εἶδος μὲν ἀριπρεπές, οὐδέ κεν ἄλλως
> οὐδὲ θεὸς τεύξειε, νόον δ' ἀποφώλιός ἐσσι.

> Stranger, <u>you have not spoken well</u>, you seem like a foolish man.
> Thus the gods do not grant pleasing gifts to all men alike
> neither form, nor mind, nor eloquence.
> For one man is lacking in beauty,
> but the god crowns him with beauty in words,
> and men look at him with delight: he <u>speaks on flawlessly</u>
> <u>with sweet modesty</u>, and is prominent among the gathered people,
> and as he goes through the city men gaze upon him as upon a god.
> Again, another resembles the immortals in shape,
> but grace is not set about his words.
> As even with you, beauty is distinct, and in no other way
> could a god himself improve it, but in mind you are reckless.

> *Odyssey* 8.166–177

Odysseus' discourse on what constitutes proper speech for a ruler is an illustration of a poetic genre referred to as "the instruction of princes," a tradition attested in Hesiod's *Works and Days* and *Theogony*.[77] Odysseus' "instruction" makes clear that a legitimate leader or ruler has "faultless speech" and "sweet modesty." In the end, after schooling Euryalus, Odysseus takes up the athletic challenge (*Odyssey* 8.185) and, as expected, he sends the discus *polu prōton* "much farther" than anyone else (*Odyssey* 8.197), a fitting wordplay with Odysseus' epithet *polutropos*. Symbolically Odysseus wins Nausicaa, as Richard Martin notes,[78] and the episode foreshadows his victory over the ill-speaking suitors in Ithaca, whose faulty discourse and behavior, like that of Euryalus, disqualify them for the kingship. Martin observes that the passage is a self-referential speech act in which Odysseus all but expressly reveals himself as king by indirectly supporting the legitimate Phaeacian heir, Laodamas, who is present during his instruction.[79] Relevant to my own study here is Martin's examination of the cognate Indo-European tradition in Old Irish royal "instruction" (*tecosc*) poetry, including the earliest (C.E. 700) attestation in *Audacht Morainn* ("Testament of Morann").[80] Finally, insofar as the physical appearance of the ruler is important, Odysseus makes clear that Euryalus, though handsome in body, is blemished in speech. The standard for the ruler ought to be higher, and of course Odysseus is the standard.

[77] Martin 1984:29–48 examines the same tradition in Hesiod, specifically in *Theogony* 79–93, where the verses 86, 91, and 92 are identical with *Odyssey* 8.71–73. In its wide attestation the so-called *speculum principum* is surveyed by West 1978:14–18.

[78] West 1984:46 "So too in Scheria there is a possibility that the new arrival [Odysseus] will knock the islanders out of contention and become Nausicaa's husband ... as it turns out, in the *Odyssey* marriage and kingship have everything to do with one another. Penelope and the rule of Ithaca are indissociable."

[79] Importantly, Martin stresses the relevance of the theme of kingship in the *Odyssey* thus: "... in Book 8, it is crucial that the audience recall Odysseus' status. Only then does one perceive that the *Odyssey* is signaling his kingship to the audience within the poem, the Phaeacians. He does so by means of prince-instruction to Euryalus" (p.44). Perhaps the rivalries for political power among oligarchs and tyrants, along with inevitable blame and praise, would have been familiar and relevant to the implied audience of Odysseus' "instruction."

[80] Kelly 1976. See also Watkins 1979. A similar composition is "Instruction of Chiron," attributed to Hesiod (frr. 283–285 M-W). An exception to the usual treatment of the *Theogony* as it relates to instruction of princes is Detienne's analysis of the work as a praise poem directed to Zeus as king (1967:17-18).

Conclusion

The intersection of the literal and the figurative meaning of the phrase *mōmon anapsai* at *Odyssey* 2.86 may be more fully understood through an intertextual and comparative approach with Irish satire from early Irish law and mythic narratives. Indeed, *mōmon anapsai* expresses the concept that language can physically hurt. The Greek evidence from Strabo 14.1.39 and the *Septuagint* Leviticus 24, as well as the assessment of relevant diction in poetic conventions of praise and blame support this argument. The phrase *mōmon anapsai* is used by Antinous to refute Telemachus' attempt "to disqualify him" (and all the suitors) as potential kings of Ithaca. To put it differently, Antinous is warning Telemachus not to blemish him ("satirize" him) and the other suitors with a flaw irreconcilable with kingship, like the disqualifying blemishes on the face of King Gaire caused by satire.

These reflexes in language of the praise-blame spectrum emphasize the suitors' dual position—at once blame poets and victims of blame. In the context of the Greek poetic tradition, the suitors' iambic sentiment is expressed through their verbal attacks, borne out of their frustration with their unsuccessful suit and bid for the kingship of Ithaca. They struggle against Penelope's delaying strategy, against Telemachus as the resisting male relative, and finally against Odysseus, the returning ruler. They transgress every rule of hospitality, they are gluttonous and greedy, they mock the good, and they are ungenerous. In addition, the suitors do not heed any warning represented by the concept of *ainos* (admonition), the space encompassing both praise and blame, like the three colors of Irish satire, each of which (black, white, and speckled) points to either the possibility or the impossibility of remediating a wrong. The suitors go beyond the pale, so to speak, and the blemish against them will stick.

The question of royal benevolence versus malevolence is the critical sociopoetic pivot in the dispensation of either praise or blame and lies at the heart of what makes a king suitable or unsuitable. In the *Odyssey*, the suitors' fitness for kingship of Ithaca is questioned, first by Telemachus' reproaches and then by Odysseus' reproaches, disguised as beggar. Odysseus tests the suitors' hospitality precisely because they are noble, just as the poet Cairpre tested king Bres.

There is never any question that Odysseus will kill the suitors for their wrongful and grievous suit, *mnēstuos argaleēs* (*Odyssey* 2.199). The suitors become the scapegoats, whose slaughter is necessary to complete the hero's last labor, so to speak. Only then can Odysseus' *nostos* be complete, and the hero reassert his role as the rightful king of Ithaca. Yet, despite the suitors' arrogance, lack of generosity toward beggars, and overall egregious behavior, the poem takes an ambivalent attitude toward their slaughter by the hero. Notwithstanding their guilt, their murder compromises Odysseus' legitimacy as king, and could raise questions about Athena's strategy for a covenant between the warring sides. After all, the suitors are the nobility of Ithaca. In this ambivalence toward Odysseus' slaughter of these men, Odysseus' and Telemachus' reputations also become blemished, even if not fatally. In the end, it is *nemesis* from the community that Odysseus must avoid, the "unrelenting bite of criticism," as Pindar puts it (*Pythian* 2.53).

In the *Odyssey*, the opposition of praise and blame marks the distance between the suitors and the heroic ideal, which in the case of Odysseus is measured especially in the hero's colossal and extraordinary knowledge of the world, experience with other peoples, and expertise in storytelling—in sum, his polytropic nature. In addition, the hero has already demonstrated his martial prowess, his *aristeia* in combat and in athletic games. In short, in every male virtue Odysseus is best. Thus, in every way the "blame of the suitors" (whether the words they utter, or the reproach leveled against them) contrasts sharply with the "praise of Odysseus," among whose fantastic deeds the most supreme are his patience, cleverness, and survival skills.

The suitors, on the other hand, lack every heroic virtue. Nevertheless, they offer the audience of the poem an opportunity to consider the apportioning of praise, blame, and cautionary tales. The suitors' mocking words take the audience into different directions as the various characters need to either obey them (slave women, the singer Phemius) because they are noble, fear them (Telemachus) because they are numerous, or suffer their insult (Odysseus as beggar). Whatever dynamics there are between the various characters and the suitors, each encounter marks them for destruction like scapegoats or sacrificial animals. Ultimately the suitors themselves fear being disqualified for kingship, and this is the sentiment Antinous expresses in his indignant and threatening response to Telemachus' censure: ἐθέλοις δέ κε μῶμον ἀνάψαι, "you wish you could blemish us" (*Odyssey* 2.86). But Telemachus is not alone in successfully "sowing blame" (*momphan epispeirōn*)—to quote Pindar's words (*Nemean* 8.39)—against the suitors. After murdering them (*Odyssey* 24.482), Odysseus is declared the king for life by Zeus himself: ὁ μὲν βασιλευέτω αἰεί, "So let him rule as a king always" (*Odyssey* 24.483).

Bibliography

Agovi, K. 1987. "Black American Dirty Dozen and the Tradition of Verbal Insult in Ghana." *Research Review in African Studies* 3:1-23.

Allan, W. 2006. "Divine Justice and Cosmic Order in Early Greek Epic." *Journal of Hellenic Studies* 126:1–35.

Allen, T. W. 1924. *Homer: The Origins and the Transmission*. Oxford.

Arndt, W. F., and W. Gingritch, eds. and trans. 1952. *A Greek-English lexicon of the New Testament, and other early Christian literature*. Chicago. Orig. pub. *Griechisch-deutsches Wörterbuch zu den Schriften des Neuen Testaments und der übrigen urchristlichen Literatur*.

Bakhtin, M. M. 1968. *Rabelais and His World*. Cambridge.

Bartelink, G. T. M. 1960. "Zur Spiritualisierung eines Opferterminus." *Glotta* 39:43–48.

Benveniste, É. 1969. *Le vocabulaire des institutions indo-européennes*. 2 vols. Paris.

Bergin, O., and R. I. Best. 1938. "Tochmarc Étaíne." *Ériu* 12:137–196.

Bond, G. W. 1952. "Archilochus and the Lycambides: A New Literary Fragment." *Hermathena* 80:2–11.

Bowra, C.M. 1961. *Greek Lyric Poetry from Alcman to Simonides*. Oxford.

Branham, R. B., ed. 2002. *Bakhtin and the Classics*. Chicago.

Breatnach, L. 2004. "On Satire and the Poet's Circuit." In *Unity in Diversity: Studies in Irish and Scottish Gaelic Language, Literature, and History*, ed. C. G. Ó. Háinle and D. Meek, 25–35. Dublin.

———. 2006. "Satire, Praise and the Early Irish Poet." *Ériu* 56:63–84.

———. 2016. "On Old Irish Collective and Abstract Nouns, the Meaning of Cétmuinter, and Marriage in Early Mediaeval Ireland." *Ériu* 66:1–29.

Bremmer, J. 1976. "Avunculate and Fosterage." *Journal of Indo-European Studies* 4:65–78.

———. 1983. "Scapegoat Rituals in Ancient Greece." *Harvard Studies in Classical Philology* 87:300–318.

Brown, C. 1989. "Ares, Aphrodite, and the Laughter of the Gods." *Phoenix* 43:283–293.

———. 2006. "Pindar on Archilochus and Gluttony of Blame (*Pyth.* 2.52-6)." *Journal of Hellenic Studies* 126:36–46.

Byre, C. S. 1988. "Penelope and the Suitors before Odysseus: *Odyssey* 18.158–303." *The American Journal of Philology* 109:159–173.

Butler, S. 1900. *The Odyssey*. London.

Ó Cathasaigh, T. 1986. "Curse and Satire." *Éigse* 21: 10–15.

Carlisle, M., and O. Levaniouk, eds. 1999. *Nine Essays on Homer*. Lanham.

Chantraine, P. 1968. *Dictionnaire etymologique de la langue grecque: histoire des mots*. Paris.

Clarke, H. W. 1963. "Telemachus and the Telemacheia." *The American Journal of Philology* 84:120–145.

Clay, J. S. 1993. "The Education of Perseus From 'Mega Nepios' to 'Dion Genos' and Back." *Materiali e discussioni per l'analisi dei testi classici* 31:23–33.

Cohn, L., P. Wendland, and S. Reiter. 1896. *Philonis Alexandrini Opera Quae Supersunt*. Vol. 5. Berlin.

Colson, F. 1937. *Philo*. Volume VII. Loeb Classical Library. Cambridge, MA.

Compton, T. M. 2006. *Victim of The Muses: Poets as Scapegoat, Warrior and Hero in Greco-Roman And Indo-European Myth And History*. Hellenic Studies Series 11. Washington, DC.

Cook, A. 1984. "Visual Aspects of the Homeric Simile in Indo-European Context." *Quaderni Urbinati di Cultura* 17:39–59.

Cullhed, E. 2006. *Eustathius Commentaries on Homer's Odyssey*. Vol. 1. Uppsala.

Cunliffe, R. J. 1963. *A Lexicon of the Homeric Dialect*. Norman.

Danek, G. 1998. *Epos und Zitat: Studien zu den Quellen der* Odyssee. Vienna.

Denniston, J. D., and K. J. Dover. 1998. *The Greek Particles*. London.

Desmidt, B. 2006. "Horn and Ivory, Bow and Scar: *Odyssey* 19.559–81." *The Classical Quarterly* 56:284–289.

Detienne. M. 1973. *Les maîtres de vérité dans la Grèce archaïque*. 2nd ed. Paris.

Dobrov, G. W. 1995. *Beyond Aristophanes: Transition and Diversity in Greek Comedy*. Atlanta.

Doederlein, L. 1850. *Homerisches Glossarium*. Vol. 1. Erlangen.

Dubois, P. 2010. *Out of Athens: The New Ancient Greeks*. Cambridge, MA.

Dumézil, G. 1943. *Servius et la Fortune: Essai sur la fonction sociale de louange et de blâme et sur les éléments indo-européens du cens romain*. Paris.

Edmunds, S. T. 1990. *Homeric Nēpios*. New York.

Elliot, R. C. 1960. *The Power of Satire: Magic, Ritual, Art*. Princeton.

Elmer, D. 2013. *The Poetics of Consent: Collective Decision Making and the* Iliad. Baltimore.

Faraone, C. A. 2004. "Hipponax Fragment 128W: Epic Parody or Expulsive Incantation?" *Classical Antiquity* 23:209–245.

Finley. M. I. 2002. *The World of Odysseus*. New York.

Floyd, E. D. 1980. "*Kleos Aphthiton*: An Indo-European Perspective on Early Greek Poetry." *Glotta* 58:133–157.

Fontenrose. J. 1960. "The Crucified Daphidas." *Transactions of the American Philological Association* 91: 83–99.

Fowler, R. L., ed. 2004. *The Cambridge Companion to Homer*. Cambridge.

Fraser, J., ed. and trans. 1916. "The First Battle of Moytura." *Ériu* 8:1–63.

Furley, W. D. 2000. " 'Fearless, Bloodless ... Like the Gods': Sappho 31 and the Rhetoric of 'Godlike.' " *The Classical Quarterly* 50:7–15.

Gerber, D. E. 1999. *Greek Iambic Poetry*. Loeb Classical Library. Harvard.

Graver, M. 1995. "Dog-Helen and Homeric Insult." *Classical Antiquity* 14:41–61.

Gray, E. A., ed. and trans. 1982. *Cath Maige Tuired: The Second Battle of Mag Tuired*. Irish Texts Society 52. Kildare.

Gwara, S. J. 1988. "Gluttony, Lust, and Penance in the B-Text of *Aislinge Meic Conglinne*." *Celtica* 20:53–72.

Gwynn, E. J. 1942. "An Old-Irish Tract on the Privileges and Responsibilities of Poets." *Ériu* 13:1–12.

Harbison, P. 2018. "Old Testament Prefigurations of New Testament Events on Irish Crosses." *Proceedings of the Royal Irish Academy: Archaeology, Culture, History, Literature, 118C*, 123–139.

Haslam, M. W. 1994. "The Homer Lexicon of Apollonius Sophista: II. Identity and Transmission." *Classical Philology* 89:107–119.

Hawkins, T. 2008. "Out-Foxing the Wolf-Walker: Lykambes as Performative Rival to Archilochus." *Classical Antiquity* 27:93–114.

Hayden, D . 2013. "Poetic Law and the Medieval Irish Linguist: Contextualizing the Vices and Virtues of Verse Composition in Auraicept na nÉces." *Language and History* 54:1034.

Heirman, J. G. M. 2012. *Space in Archaic Greek Lyric: City, Countryside and Sea*. PhD diss., University of Amsterdam.

Hercher, R. 1864. *Claudii Aeliani de natura animalium libri xvii, varia historia, epistolae, fragmenta*. Vol. 1. Leipzig.

Hildburgh, W. L. 1946. "Apotropaism in Greek Vase-Paintings." *Folklore* 57:154–178.

Hodgart, M. J. C. 2010. *Satire: Origins and Principles*. New Brunswick.

Hornblower, S., and A. Spawforth, eds. 1996. *The Oxford Classical Dictionary*. Oxford.

Hull, V. 1930. "Cairpre mac Edaine's Satire upon Bres mac Eladain." *Zeitschrift für Celtische Philologie* 18:63–69.

Isenberg, M. 1975. "The Sale of Sacrificial Meat." *Classical Philology* 70:271–273.

Jackson, K. H., ed. 1990. *Aislinge Meic Con Glinne*. Dublin.

Johnstone, H. 1997. "A Fragment of Simonides?" *The Classical Quarterly* 47:293–295.

Jones, S. S. 1976. "'The Rarest Thing in the World': Indo-European or African?" *Research in African Literatures* 7:200–210.

Joynt, M., ed. 1931. *Tromdámh Guaire*. Mediaeval and Modern Irish Series 2. Dublin.

Kelly, F. 1976. ed. and tr. *Audacht Morainn*. Dublin.

———. 1988. *A Guide to Ancient Irish Law*. Dublin

Kirk, G. S. 1962. *The Songs of Homer*. Cambridge.

———. 1976. *Homer and the Oral Tradition*. Cambridge.

Kohnken, A. 1981. "Apollo's Retort to Envy's Criticism: (Two Questions of Relevance in Callimachus, Hymn 2,105FF)." *American Journal of Philology* 102:411–422.

Koster, W. J. W., and Holwerda, D. 1969. *Scholia in Aristophanem*. Bouma.

Kouklanakis, A. 1999. "Thersites, Odysseus, and the Social Order." In Carlisle and Levaniouk 1999:35-53.

———. 2016. "From Cultural Appropriation to Historical Emendation: Two Case Studies of Reception of the Classical Tradition in Brazil." In *Receptions of the Classics in the African Diaspora of the Hispanophone and Lusophone Worlds*, ed. E. G. Rizo and M. M. Henry, 9-30. Lanham.

Lateiner, D. 1998. *Sardonic Smile: Nonverbal Behavior in Homeric Epic*. Ann Arbor.

Liddell, H. G., R. Scott, and H.S. Jones. 1996. *Greek-English Lexicon*. Oxford.

Lincoln, B. 1989. *Discourse and the Construction of Society: Comparative Studies of Myth, Ritual, and Classification*. New York.

Lord, A. B. 1960. *The Singer of Tales*. Cambridge, MA.

Lowry, E. R. 1991. *Thersites: A Study in Comic Shame*. New York.

Lucas, F. L. 1968. *Greek Tragedy and Comedy*. New York.

Maiullari, F. 2003. "La mosca, un parodistico simbolo del doppio in Omero (Ovvero, la mosca e Tersite)." *Quaderni Urbinati di Cultura Classica* 74:33–68.

Marks, J. 2005. "The Ongoing *Neikos*: Thersites, Odysseus, and Achilleus." *American Journal of Philology* 126:1–31.

Martin, R. P. 1989. *The Language of Heroes: Speech and Performance in the* Iliad. Ithaca, NY.

———. 1984. "Hesiod, Odysseus, and the Instruction of Princes," *Transactions of the American Philological Association* 114: 29–48.

Martinazzoli, F. *Hapax legomenon, Parte prima (II): Il lexicon Homericum di Apollonio Sofista*. Bari.

Masson, O. 1987. *Les fragments du poète Hipponax*. New York.

Matthews, J. 1998. *The Bardic Source Book: Inspirational Legacy and Teachings of the Ancient Celts*. London.

Mazon, P. 1942. *Introduction à l'Iliade*. Paris.

McKenna, C. 2005. "Vision and Revision, Iteration and Reiteration, in Aislinge Meic Con Glinne." *Heroic Poets and Poetic Heroes in Celtic Tradition. A Festschrift for Patrick K. Ford*, ed. J. F. Nagy and L. E. Jones, 269–282.

Merkelbach, R., and M. L West. 1970. *Hesiodi Opera*. Repr. 1990. Oxford.

———. 1967. *Fragmenta Hesiodea*. Oxford.

Merry, W. W. 1987. *Homer's* Odyssey. New York.

Meyer, K. 1907. *Anecdota from Irish Manuscripts*. Dublin.

Mhaoldomhnaigh, A. 2007. *Satirical Narrative in Early Irish Literature*. PhD diss., NUI Maynooth.

Miralles, C., and J. Pòrtulas. 1983. *Archilochus and the Iambic Poetry*. Rome.

Monro, D. B. 1901. *Homer's* Odyssey. Oxford.

Montanari, F. 2006. "Daphitas." In *Brill's New Pauly*, ed. H. Cancik and H. Schneider. http://dx.doi.org/10.1163/1574-9347_bnp_e310790.

Mooney, G. W. 1912. *Commentary on* Argonautica. London.

Muellner, L. 1976. *The Meaning of Homeric* Eukhomai *through Its Formulas*. Innsbruck.

Murray. A. T. 1995. *The Odyssey*. Loeb Classical Library. 2 vols. Harvard.

Nagler, M. 1990. "Odysseus: The Proem and the Problem." *Classical Antiquity* 9:335–356

Nagy, G. 1979. *The Best of the Achaeans: Concepts of the Hero in Archaic Greek Poetry*. Baltimore.

———. 1990. *Pindar's Homer: The Lyric Possession of an Epic Past*. Baltimore. 1994.

———. 1996. *Poetry as Performance: Homer and Beyond*. Cambridge.

———. 1996. *Homeric Questions*. Austin.

———. 2004. *Homer's Text and Language*. Urbana.

Ogden, D. 1993. "Cleisthenes of Sicyon, Λευστήρ." *The Classical Quarterly* 43:353–363.

Pache, C. 1999. "Odysseus and the Phaeacians." In Carlisle and Levaniouk 1999:21–33.

Padel, R. 1994. *In and out of the Mind: Greek Images of the Tragic Self*. Princeton.

Page, D. L. 1955. *The Homeric Odyssey*. Oxford.

Pagliai, V. 2009. "The Art of Dueling with Words: Toward a New Understanding of Verbal Duels across the World." *Oral Tradition* 24:61–88.

Parkes, P. 2004. "Fosterage, Kinship, and Legend: When Milk Was Thicker Than Blood?" *Comparative Studies in Society and History* 46:587–615.

Parry, A. A. 1973. *Blameless Aegisthus: A Study of ἀμύμων and Other Homeric Epithets*. Leiden.

Parry, A. 1971. *The Making of Homeric Verse: The Collected Papers of Milman Parry*. Oxford.

Pfeiffer, R. 1968. *History of Classical Scholarship from the Beginnings to the End of the Hellenistic Age*. Oxford.

Qiu, F. 2014. "Narratives in Early Irish Law Tracts." PhD diss., University College Cork.

Rihll, T. E. 1989. "Lawgivers and Tyrants (Solon, Fr. 9–11 West)." *The Classical Quarterly* 39:277–286.

Robertson, N. 1969. "How to Behave at a Sacrifice: Hesiod *Erga* 755–56." *Classical Philology* 64:164–169.

Rosen, R. M. 1988a. "Hipponax and the Homeric Odysseus." *Eikasmos* 1:11–25.

———. 1988b. "Hipponax, Boupalos, and the Conventions of *Psogos*." *Transactions of the American Philological Association* 111:29–41.

———. 2003. "The Death of Thersites and the Sympotic Performance of Iambic Mockery." *Pallas* 61:121–136.

———. 2007. *Making Mockery: The Poetics of Ancient Satire.* New York.

Rotstein, A. 2010. *The Idea of* Iambos. Oxford.

Russell, P. 2008. "Poets, Power and Possessions in Medieval Ireland: Some Stories from *Sanas Cormaic*." In *Law, Literature, and Society*, ed. J. F. Eska. CSANA Yearbook 7:9–45. Dublin.

Saïd, S. 1979. "Les crimes des prétendants: La maison d'Ulysse et les festin de l'*Odyssée*." *Études de littérature ancienne* 1:9–49.

Samaras, P. P. 1996. "Ἔρως τυραννίδος": *A Study of the Representations in Greek Lyric Poetry of the Powerful Emotional [sic] Response That Tyranny Provoked in Its Audience at the Time of Tyranny's Earliest Appearance in the Ancient World.* MA thesis, McGill University.

Seidensticker, B. 1978. "Archilochus and Odysseus." *Greek, Roman, and Byzantine Studies* 19:5–22.

Shercliff, R. 2015. "Textual Correspondences in *Tochmarc Ferbe*." *Proceedings of Harvard Celtic Colloquium* 35:187–203.

Smith, W. D. 1966. "Physiology in the Homeric poems." *Transactions and Proceedings of the American Philological Association* 97:547–56.

Steiner, D. 1986. *The Crown of Song: Metaphor in Pindar.* New York.

———. 2009. "Diverting Demons: Ritual, Poetic Mockery and the Odysseus-Iros Encounter." *Classical Antiquity* 28:72–100.

Steinrück, M. 2008. *The Suitors in the* Odyssey: *The Clash Between Homer and Archilochus.*

Stokes, W. 1862. *Three Irish Glossaries: Sanas Cormaic's Glossary.* London.

———. 1868, 1903. "The Wooing of Luaine and Death of Athirne." *Revue Celtique* 24:270-287.

———. 1887. "The Seige of Howth." *Revue Celtique* 8: 47-64.

———. 1891. "The Second Battle of Moytura." *Revue Celtique* 12:52–130.

———. 1910. "Tidings of Conchobar Mac Nessa." *Ériu* 4:18-38.

Taplin, O. 2009. "Pots & Plays. Interactions between Tragedy and Greek Vase-Painting of the Fourth Century B.C." *Gnomon* 81:439–447.

———. 2014. "How Pots and Papyri Might Prompt a Re-Evaluation of Fourth-Century Tragedy." In *Greek Theatre in the Fourth Century BC*, ed. E. Csapo, H. R. Goette, J. R. Green, and P. Wilson, 141-156. Berlin.

Test, G. A. 1991. *Satire: Spirit and Art*. Tampa.

Thalmann, W .G. 1988. "Thersites: Comedy, Scapegoats, and Heroic Ideology in the *Iliad*." *Transactions of the American Philological Association* 118:1–28.

Thomas, C. G. 1988. "Penelope's Worth: Looming Large in Early Greece." *Hermes* 116:257–264.

Vagnone, G. 1990. "Cautela e disattenzione nell' "Odissea": La rovina (ὄλεθρος) dei Proci." *Quaderni Urbinati di Cultura Classica* 34:145–150.

Vahlen, J., R. Helm, et al. 1911. *Gesammelte Philologische Schriften*. Leipzig.

Vallozza, M. 1989. "Il motivo dell'invidia in Pindaro." *Quaderni Urbinati di Cultura Classica* 31:13–30.

Vodoklys, E. J. 1992. *Blame-Expression in the Epic Tradition*. New York.

Watkins, C. 1962. "Varia. II." *Ériu* 19:114-118.

———. 1995. *How to Kill a Dragon: Aspects of Indo-European Poetics*. Oxford.

West, M. L. 1974. *Studies in Greek Elegy and Iambus*. New York.

———. 1978. *Hesiod. Works and Days*. Oxford.

———. 2003. *Greek Epic Fragments*. Loeb Classical Library. Harvard.

Whitfield. 2016. "Aristocratic Display in Early Medieval Ireland in Fiction and in Fact: The Dazzling White Tunic and Purple Cloak" *Peritia* 27:173–174.

Wiedemann, T. E. J. 1981. *Greek and Roman Slavery*. London.

Wilamowitz-Moellendorff, U. V. 1924. *Hellenistische Dichtung in der Zeit des Kallimachos*. Berlin.

Williams, B. A. O. 1993. *Shame and Necessity*. Berkeley.

Williams, F. 1978. *Callimachus:* Hymn to Apollo; *A Commentary*. Oxford.

Worman, N. 2008. *Abusive Mouths in Classical Athens*. New York.

Index of Non-English Terms

Greek

adēlōn, 69
aeikeliōs, 24n7; *aeikēs*, 24n7; *aeikizein*, 24n7
aergoi, 76
aethloi, 47
agalmata, 65
agatha, 43
agenneis, 77n56
agōn, 42n5, 45, 46, 47, 49, 84
agoreuōn, 40n48
aidēla, 74, 75; *aidēlon*, 74, 75
aidoiēis, 52
ainos, 4n7, 13, 14, 15, 18, 38, 52, 64, 83, 87
aipun, 43
aiskhea, 25; *aiskhunōn*, 59, 62
aitian, 63; *aitioi*, 81
akēlidōton, 68
akosma, 26
alokhoisin, 52
amōmos, 68, 69, 70; *amumōn*, 8n16, 69, 70; *amumonos*, 70, 79n65
anaidēisi, 8
anapsai, 1, 5, 7, 26, 29n20, 30, 59, 60, 61, 62, 63, 65, 66, 70, 73, 75, 87; *anaptō*, 60, 61, 62, 65, 66, 70
anatithēmi, 65
anax, 30
anēr, 1n1, 25n11
anupaitiou, 68

aoidos, 25n10
aphanizō, 74n46
argaleēs, 41, 88
Argeiphontes, 42
aristēes, 46; *aristeia*, 51, 88; *aristoi*, 1n1, 57
ateleia, 26; *atelēs*, 25, 35
anabainō, 61

basileis, 1n1, 4, 8, 9, 10, 16, 21, 29n20, 30, 57; *basilēos*, 70, 79n65; *basileus*, 9, 16n41, 20, 40, 63; *basileusin*, 67n22, 69, 70, 77n57; *basileutatos*, 1n1; *basileuteros*, 1n1
biē, 24n5
bōmolokhia, 56, 75

dapsen, 64
diakrinai, 47; *dikastēs*, 29n20; *distikhos*, 70n34
dōdekaton, 19, 31n25
doliois, 80n68
dolophroneōn, 80n68
dusphamon, 64

edontes, 29, 52, 75
ekhōn, 29
ekhthra, 21; *ekhthros*, 19n54, 20, 21, 36n35, 55
ektanon, 54
elenkhea, 81n70

epainos, 6, 83n72
epeessi, 80n68
epimnēstheis, 43
epispeirōn, 64, 88
epistamenōs, 25n10
epōn, 66; *epos*, 24, 35n32, 36, 40, 78
eranos, 18
erasmon, 55
erizemenai, 30n22, 34n31, 63n14
ērkhe, 43
eterpon, 54
ēthos, 64

gambroi, 47
gameō, 44; *gamon*, 46; *gamos*, 51
gasteri margēi, 28n18
geloios, 25
grammatikos, 70, 70n33

haimatoessa, 73n42
hapsidas, 66; *hapsis*, 66; *hapsis*, 66
haptetai, 63n13, 64
haptō, 60, 61, 61n6, 62, 62n9, 62n10,
    63n11, 66; *haptomai*, 65, 66, 76n55
hēmeas, 62
herma poleōs, 1n1, 57
hetairoi, 19, 20n57, 55, 56, 56n27
hezeto, 16
holokautos, 68
horkōi, 35
hubristai, 43; *hubrizontes*, 18
huperphialoi, 8, 84; *huperphialōs*, 18
huphainō, 66n19
hupodmētheisa, 50n18
hupsagorē, 31, 60
hupsos, 60n5

kakoxeinos, 34
Kāmaduh, 9
kertomia, 70
khoinikos, 61n7; *khoinix*, 61n7
khoron, 47
khreos, 62n9

kleinos, 49
kleos, 8, 13, 14, 38, 64, 65n17
kleptosunēi, 35
kōmos, 56, 56n27
kudos, 65, 65n10
kuōn, 18n51; *kunōpēs*, 18n51

lōbē, 24, 25, 68, 70; *lōbētēr*, 25
loidorēsanta, 70; *loidoria*, 72
lugrōi, 64

makhēs, 49
memōlōpismenon, 78n37
memphomai, 70
mempsis, 64n16
menein, 60n3
menos, 39, 39n47, 59n3, 60n3, 60n4
minutheskon, 52
mnaasthai, 43, 44; *mnaomai*, 43,
    53; *mnastēres*, 46, 47; *mnēsato*,
    43; *mnēstēis*, 52; *mnēstēn*,
    44, 51; *mnēstēroktonia*,
    51n20; *mnēstēroktonos*, 51;
    mnēstērophonia, 51, 51n20, 79, 81;
    mnēstuos, 41, 88; *mnēstus*, 41
mōlōpas, 7n36; *mōlōpes*, 71, 72, 73,
    73n42; *mōlōpes porphureoi*, 71, 72,
    73, 73n42; *mōlōpizō*, 72; *mōlōps*, 67
mōmaomai, 43, 70; *mōmar*, 49;
    mōmeomai, 70; *mōmeuō*, 70, 73
mōmos, 6, 9, 12, 13, 25, 31n25, 33,
    49, 59, 59n2, 61, 62, 63, 63n13,
    66, 67, 67n23-24, 68, 69, 69n28,
    70, 70n30, 73, 75, 80, 81, 83n72;
    mōmos-phthonos, 75
momphan, 64, 88; *momphē*, 64n16;
    momphos, 64n16
morphē epeōn, 25n10
muthōn, 43; *muthos*, 25n9, 25n10,
    35n32, 42, 52, 85

neikei, 64; *neikos*, 24, 25,
nemesaō, 83; *nemesis*, 81, 82, 83, 88

nēpios, 8, 35, 36, 36n37, 36n38, 39, 39n47, 40, 40n48

ōkumoroi, 50
olethron, 43; *olethrou*, 61
ololugē, 79
oneidea, 70; *oneidizō*, 43; *oneidos*, 13, 25

parthenoi alphesiboiai, 27n13
peirēsesthai, 44n9
pepnumenos, 39n47
pharmakon, 77n56; *pharmakos*, 77n56
phasganōi, 64
phēmis, 81n70
philomōmos, 83n72
philopsogos, 83, 83n72
philos, 19n54, 55, 56n27
philotēs, 28
phrenes esthlai, 25n10
phrenōn, 66; *phroneōn*, 43
Phthonos, 31n25, 75, 84
pikrogamoi, 50
podōn, 47
poiētēs, 70n33,
poleōs, 1n1, 57
polu proton, 85, 86
polumētis, 35, 35n33
polutropos, 85, 86
Polynoe, 69n26
porphureoi, 71, 72, 73, 73n42; *porphureos*, 72n40
pros-haptō, 62, 63n11
protiaptō, 62, 62n10, 65
psegō, 13n33,
psogeros, 25
psogon, 14, 14n37, 18, 27n14, 56

sarkazō, 32, 32n28, 32n29
skoteinon, 27n14
smōdix, 73n42; *smodix haimatoessa*, 73n42
sussitia, 56

teleios, 25, 40n49, 69n28, 70, 79; *teleioteron*, 68, 69
tharsaleōs, 31, 36n39; *tharsos*, 23n4, 24n4
tukhēi, 63

xeinos, 21, 27n14, 84n75

Irish
áer, 2, 3, 5, 10, 11n24, 11n27, 12n29, 24, 73, 76
ail, 73n43
ailche, 73n43
ainim, 5, 10, 11
anaid, 73n43
antar, 73n43

boulgae, 4, 11

ferb, 5n12, 11, 78, 94
fili, 3, 71

glam dicend, 5, 11, 70n34

molad 3, 3n3, 3n4, 5

tecosc, 86

Latin
accusare, 43

impetus, 38n44
infans, 36

notare, 66n21

verbum, 11, 78
vir, 25n11

Subject Index

abuse(s), 24-25, 28n19, 33, 56, 62n10

Achelous, 47, 48, 49

Achilles, 1n1, 23n2, 24n7, 51n20, 62, 79n62

Áed (person), 4n9

Aegisthus, 38-39, 41-43, 44, 44n4, 50, 52, 65

Agamemnon, 1n1, 17n46, 23n2, 28, 30n22, 41, 41n1, 41n3, 42-43, 45, 50, 51, 52, 61n6, 65

Alcinous, 27, 67n22, 76n54, 82

Antinous, 1, 8, 16, 18n48, 20-21, 23, 26-28, 29n20, 30n22, 31-33, 31n25, 34, 34n30, 35, 36, 46, 54-56, 57, 59, 59n3, 60, 60n4, 65, 66, 70, 75, 76n53, 80-81, 84n76, 87, 88

Archilochus, 12n28, 14, 16, 17-18, 19, 19n53, 20, 20n53, 26, 55, 56n27, 57n30, 77n56

Aristotle, 1n1, 13-16, 19, 56n27, 65; Aristotelian, 16n40

Atalanta, 44, 50, 51

Athenaeus, 17n47, 51n20, 71n36

Athirne, 4n10, 12n30, 44n8, 73n43. See also "Wooing of Luaine and the Death of Athirne"

Audacht Morainn, 86

bard(s), 13n34

Bacchylides, 18-19, 40n50, 67n23

beggar-stranger, 21

blame poetics, 1-2,12n32,23n2, 67; blame poetry, 13-14, 16, 18, 23, 32, 41-43, 55, 56n27, 70

blemish(es), 4, 13n33, 59, 59, 62, 65, 67, 67n24, 68, 68n24, 72, 73, 73n42, 73n43, 87

brand (set a brand), 5, 12n28, 25, 59-69, 66

Bres Mac Eladain (king), 9

bruise(s), 71, 71n36, 72

Bupalus, 77n56

Caier. See Gaire

Cairpre Mac Edaine (poet), 9, 12n29, 87

Callimachus, 31n25, 75

Cath Maige Tuired, 4n9, 12n29, 12n30

Charilaus, 55

chariot-race, 46, 49

Clytemnestra, 41, 43-44, 45n12, 50-51, 52

comparandum, 2, 40, 44n8

courtship, 27, 41, 51. See also woo/ wooing

Conchobar (king), 4n10; Conchobar-cycle, 5n11

Connacht, 4n9

Ctesippus, 20n57, 24

Cuindgedach, 12

Dállan, 4n9

Daphitas, 70, 70n32, 71, 72, 72n41, 93

Deianeira, 47, 49, 50n18
Deipnosophistai, 17n47
Demeter, 20, 21
Detienne, Marcel, 5-6, 65n17, 86n80
Diodorus Siculus, 13n34
Dionysus of Halicarnassus, 71, 71n36, 72
disfigure, 62; disfigurement, 25
distich, 70-72
druid(s), 13n34
Dumézil, Georges, 2, 3, 3n5, 4, 5, 5n13, 9, 9n20, 11, 13, 19, 39n45, 83n73; *Vache d'Abondance* 9, 10n20

enslavement/enslaved people, 52, 71-72
Erinyes, 49
Eurycleia, 8, 39n47, 57, 78, 79
Eurynome, 21n58
Eustathius, 31n26, 32, 51n20

famine-demons, 77, 79
feast(s)/feasting, 17-18, 26, 30, 33, 35, 53, 55, 56, 68n24, 73, 78
First Battle of Moytura, 9n19
flaw(s), 10n23, 13n33, 26, 31, 87

Gaire, 5n11, 10, 10n21, 11, 12, 12n29, 87
Guaire, 4n9, 40
guest-host, 25n10, 27

Halitherses, 54
hapax legomenon, 59, 59n2
Hector, 24n6, 24n7, 49, 51n21
Heracles, 28n16, 38n43, 47-49, 57n28
Hesiod, 19n52, 29n20, 40, 44, 44n9, 45, 50, 50n17, 66, 69n26, 73, 74, 74n45, 86, 86n77, 86n80; *Catalogue of Women*, 44n9, 45, 50
highfalutin, 32
Hipponax, 12n32, 36n35, 77, 78, 80n67
Homer, 16n40, 24n7, 25, 26, 29n20, 31n26, 35, 36n39, 46, 56n27, 59,

62, 63n15, 66, 70, 70n30, 70n32, 74; Homeric formula, 77n60; *Homeric Hymn to Demeter*, 20-21; Homeric poetry, 8, 62
honor-price, 4
hospitality, 7, 8, 9, 27n15, 33, 41n2, 87

Iambe, 20, 20n57, 21, 21n59
iambeiophagos, 18n48
iambic poetry, 12n28, 13, 17, 17n45, 19-21, 20n57, 51, 59, 77n56, 87
illegitimate, 10, 40
ill-fated, 41
Indic, 2, 19, 21, 39n45
Indo-European, 86
insult(s)/insulting, 4, 7, 18n48, 18n51, 20, 24, 25, 28, 30, 33, 51, 54, 55-56, 57n30, 70, 72, 72n41, 73n43, 77n56, 83, 85, 88
Irish literature, 4n7, 12n31, 13n34, 40, 73n43, 71n35, 72n40, 86; old Irish, 11, 86; Irish satire (*see under* satire)
ironic, 31, 32n29, 33, 80
Irus, 28n18, 56
Ithaca 1, 4, 7, 21, 30, 33, 36, 38, 41, 51, 70, 78, 81, 84, 86, 86n78, 87, 88

judgment, 11, 17, 18n48, 29n20

Kāmaduh, 9

Laodamas, 27, 86
Latin, 11, 12n29, 25n11, 36, 38n44, 43, 66n21, 78
law, 2, 3, 3n4, 5, 73n43, 87; daughter(s)-in law, 52; father(s)-in law, 19, 20; son (s)-in-law, 46-47, 52
Leocritus, 55
legitimate, 3, 82-84, 86
lowborn, 72n41
Luaine, 4n10, 5n11, 12n30, 44n8

Lycambes, 19, 20, 20n56, 56n27, 77n56
Lysianassa, 69n26

magic, 5, 9, 12n29, 40, 49, 66
Margites, 13-14, 15, 15n38, 15n39, 16, 28n18, 37n40
marriage, 20, 30, 42n4, 44-46, 48-49, 50, 51, 52, 59n1, 65, 79, 81, 82-84, 86n78
Momus, 29n20
mythopoetic, 10n20, 51

Nagy, Gregory, 13-14, 16n40, 18n50, 23n1, 28n18, 56n27
Néide mac Adnai, 4n9, 10, 10n21
nonverbal, 57n20

Odysseus, 1n1, 4, 4n10, 7-9, 13, 16-17, 18, 18n51, 19, 20n56, 20n57, 21, 23, 24, 25n10, 26, 27-28, 29, 30n22, 31n24, 33, 35, 36, 37, 37n41, 37n42, 28, 39n45, 39n47, 41, 44n9, 45n11, 47, 51, 51n20, 52, 52n22, 54-55, 57, 59, 60n5, 61, 65, 67, 73n42, 75, 75n49, 76, 77n57, 78, 79, 80n68, 82, 84, 85, 86, 86n78, 86n79, 87, 88
Oenomaus, 49, 49n15, 51, 51n20
Oenopion, 49, 51

Penelope, 5, 7, 8, 10, 16, 18n51, 20, 21n58, 21n59, 26, 27-28, 28n17, 29, 30, 39n47, 40, 41, 43-44, 44n9, 45, 51, 52, 54, 55n26, 66, 67n22, 75, 76, 76n53, 80, 81-82, 84, 84n76, 85, 86n78, 87
Pericles, 17, 18
Phaeacian(s), 25n10, 27, 60n5, 76n54, 82, 83, 84, 86
Philo, 68, 69, 70
Pindar, 14, 17-18, 18n49, 19, 19n54, 23n2, 26, 27n14, 28n18, 31n25,

45, 46, 47, 47n14, 49n15, 50-51, 56n27, 61n6, 62n10, 63, 63n14, 64-65, 67n23, 83n72, 83n74, 88
poet(s), 3, 3n4, 4, 4n10, 5n11, 12n28, 12n29, 13n34, 17, 21, 23, 28 and n18, 40, 55, 63, 67, 71n35, 73n43, 87
polytropic, 21, 88
praise-blame, 87
praise-poem/poetry, 3n3, 14, 18, 86n80; praise-satire, 4
Pr̥thu, 2, 9
purple-striped, 71-73

reproach(es), 4, 7, 8, 9, 10n22, 21, 23, 24, 24n6, 25, 28-29, 30, 31n25, 41, 43, 51, 54, 55, 59-60, 62n10, 64, 66, 67, 70, 73, 81-84, 87, 88
ritual, 17n45, 70, 77, 77n56, 77n60, 78-79
royal, 1n1, 2, 4-5, 10, 31n24, 39n45, 40, 72, 73n41, 78, 86, 87

Sanas Cormaic, 3n3, 10, 11
Sanskrit, 9
satire, 2, 4, 6, 12n28, 36, 44, 65, 66n21, 67, 70, 72, 76, 87; Irish satire, 2-6, 9-12, 11n27, 21, 32-33, 44n8, 59, 65, 67, 73n43, 76, 87
scapegoat, 12n32, 17n45, 76-77, 78-79, 78n61, 88
Second Battle of Moytura, 9
Septuagint, 67n23, 67n24, 68, 87
slavery/slaves. *See* enslavement/ enslaved people
speculum principum, 86n77
speech(es), 1, 13-14, 16, 25n10, 41-43, 50, 51-52, 63-4, 63n14, 82-83, 83n72, 85-86; speech act, 13, 86; and the suitors, 1, 16-17, 23, 26, 32-33, 54-55, 65; and Telemachus, 32, 36, 39, 54-55, 75
stigma, 84

Strabo, 51n20, 70-71, 72, 72n41, 73,
    77n65, 81n69, 87
swift-footed, 44, 50

Theognis, 16n40, 18
Thersites, 1, 1n41, 1n43, 17, 23, 24n4,
    25, 26, 28, 29, 30n27, 34n31,
    51n20, 63n14, 63n15, 73n42
Thersitoktonos vase, 51n20
thin-skinned, 73n41
trefocal, 3-4, 13n25
Tromdámh Guaire, 4n9
Tuatha Dé Danann, 9, 12n31

Underworld, 65

woo/wooing, 7, 26, 30, 41-44, 44n9,
    45, 45n12, 50-53, 71n53; wooed-
    and-won 42, 43
"The Wooing of Luaine and the Death
    of Athirne," 5n11, 12n30, 44n8
wrongdoing, 9, 18, 29, 77

Zeus, 29n20, 38, 41, 42n4, 43, 44n9, 48,
    50, 51-52, 62, 64, 78, 80-81, 84n75,
    86n80, 88